Second Chances

Six sexy stories about getting a second shot at the gold ring

"Back to School" -- An admin error forces Jordan and Dennis to share a dorm room. Older than their classmates, they decide to stick together. But Jordan's past threatens to keep them apart.

"Gordon" -- When the cover model of her latest book walks into the coffee shop where she writes, Lenore embarrassingly calls him by her character's name. His reaction confounds her.

"Spa Date" -- Dismayed that she introduced Sam to the woman who betrayed her, Julie tries to fix her up again.

"Salt for His Wounds" -- When Eleanor's ex-husband shows up begging for a second chance, she asks her young, gorgeous next door neighbor for a favor. Mick takes advantage of the opportunity.

"Proposal -- Tangled Webs" -- The evening appears perfectly arranged for him to pop the question. But, Christopher's proposition takes Geraldine on an unanticipated sexual adventure.

"Starting Over" -- When her pet walked out on her, she stayed away from parties because it hurt to watch other women playing with their toys. But, a friend coerces her into attending a unique event.

I.G. Frederick trades words for cash, specializing in erotic fiction and poetry since 2001. Her erotic short stories appear in Hustler Fantasies, Forum, Foreplay, and Desire Presents, as well as electronic, audio, and print anthologies. Her novels receive high praise from readers, critics, and other authors.

A FemDom, Ms. Frederick, owns the man she adores. Although dominant in the rest of his life, he demonstrates his love by serving as her submissive. Ms. Frederick often writes about finding love in BDSM relationships from the authority of one enjoying that for almost a decade.

http://eroticawriter.net/

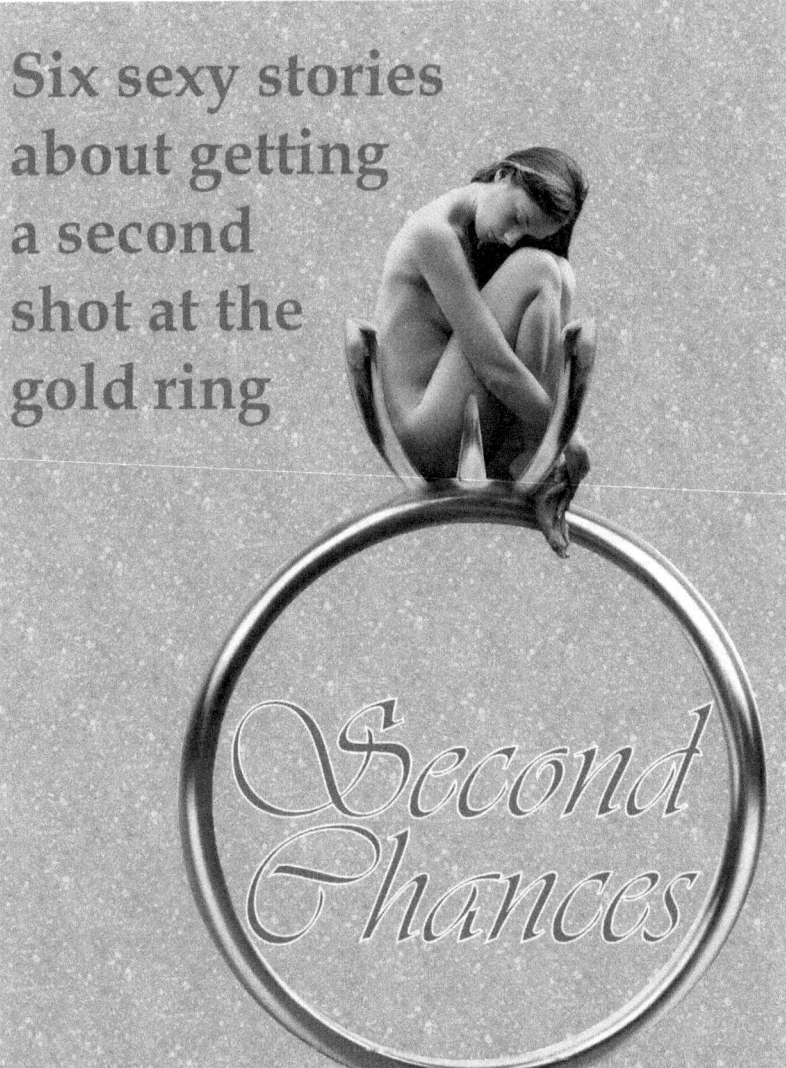

Six sexy stories
about getting
a second
shot at the
gold ring

Second Chances

I.G. Frederick
Author of Cougar Conquests

Second Chances
© **2014 by I.G. Frederick**

ISBN: 978-1937471-23-1

Pussy Cat Press
http://pussycatpress.com/publisher.html/
P.O. Box 19764
Portland OR 97280

First published electronically in 2013

"Starting Over" (condensed) published by *Forum*, July, 2008
"Salt for his Wounds" previously published in Midnight
Showcase's *Sweet Revenge* anthology, September, 2005

This book is a work of fiction. The names, characters, places,
and incidents are products of the writer's imagination or
have been used fictitiously and are not to be construed as
real. Any resemblance to persons living or dead, actual
events, locale or organizations is entirely coincidental.

Table of Contents

Back to School

By I.G. Frederick

Jordan leaned on her battered Civic trying to catch her breath. "One more." Her words turned to fog. The temperature had dropped twenty degrees since sundown. Despite the exertion of unloading everything she owned and dragging it up two flights of stairs, she shivered.

The sooner she deposited the last box in the tiny room, the sooner she could take a hot shower and collapse, she told herself.

Balancing the box on her hip, she fumbled with her keys trying to unlock the entrance to the seven-story, yellow brick building she would call home for the next six months to two years. Shoving the box on top of the others she'd stacked at the foot of the bunk beds, she wondered about the woman who would share her room and life for the term. Probably some young pretty thang straight out of high school with a stunning figure and a line of athletes queuing up to compete for the right to take her out.

Jordan dug a towel and the zipped plastic bag with what

was left of the toiletries from the shelter out of the suitcase she'd dumped on one of the two desks built onto the wall opposite the bunk beds. Trudging through the long hallway to the women's washroom, which of course was at the opposite end of the building, she passed hunky guys and gorgeous gals and wished she were almost anywhere else.

She found an empty shower stall, stripped out of her stained shirt and torn jeans, and stood under the hot water for a full five minutes before she even dug out shampoo. Clean hair and warmed skin improved her disposition, but not her exhaustion. She wrapped the towel around herself, folded it above her almost non-existent breasts, and gathered up her stinky clothing.

Back in her room, which still showed no evidence of another occupant, she tossed her laundry on top of her stack of boxes, crawled into the upper bunk, pulled the sheet over her face, and burrowed under the blankets.

The next thing she knew, men's voices in her ear startled her from the sleep of the dead. She peaked out from under the covers to see three guys dumping green sea bags in the middle of the floor.

"Looks like your roomie already took over the joint," the tallest one said.

"Don't worry, I'll set him straight," one said with a slow Southern drawl. "Probably some spoiled young punk." Although an inch shorter than the first speaker, he still stood better than six feet tall. He had cropped black hair and wore a Navy sweatshirt, faded blue jeans, and shiny black deck boots.

Jordan was stark naked and her room had been invaded by the basketball team. She screamed.

"Whoa, dude, you didn't tell us you'd already found yourself a dame and stashed her back here," one said.

"What's your roomie gonna think about you occupyin' both bunks?" This from the previously silent third male, a head shorter than the other two with shoulder-length dreads and full sleeve tattoos.

"Excuse me, Ma'am," the Navy sweatshirt said. "May I ask why you're in my room?"

"Your room?" Jordan shrieked. "This is my room and if the three of you don't get out of here immediately, I'm calling security." Of course the only phone was on the desk and she was trapped, naked, in her bed. But they didn't know that.

"You don't have to pretend old Dennis didn't know you were here." Tats punched "Dennis" in the shoulder.

Jordan sucked in her breath, prepared to scream until someone heard and came to investigate. Dennis grabbed his two friends by the biceps and turned them toward the door. "Thanks for helping me with my gear, fellows. I think you'd better let me talk to the Lady here and find out what's going on."

Outside, one of them turned with mouth open, but Dennis shut the door.

"You can go with them." Jordan pulled the bedding down to her neck.

"I would, Ma'am, but then I'd have nowhere to sleep tonight."

Jordan just stared at him.

"This is my room, Ma'am. If you're sure it's yours then there must have been some type of mistake."

He held his hand up to her level. "I'm Dennis. Not the best circumstances to meet under, perhaps, but I'm pleased to make your acquaintance."

Jordan stuck one hand out from under her blankets while clutching them around her neck with the other. "Jordan."

A smile twitched at the corners of Dennis' lips as he shook her hand.

Jordan shut her eyes. She'd written "female" in capital letters on every form she'd filled out.

"I'm guessing you've run into this type of problem before?"

She sighed. Getting mail addressed to "Mr." and having callers ask to speak to her husband didn't compare to getting stuck with a male roommate.

"If you could bear with me for one night, Miss Jordan, I'll be happy to go down to administration and get this straightened out in the morning."

She rolled her eyes. Won't be anyone there tomorrow. Saturday."

He tilted his head, allowing her to see his eyes were bright blue and that they had just a hint of wrinkles around them as if he often squinted. "Even though it's orientation?"

She nodded. "Apparently administration doesn't participate in orientation, just academics."

"I suppose if I promise to be the perfect gentleman you won't be comfortable sharing a room for the weekend?" He held out his hands palm up. "I assure you I'm harmless, at least where women are concerned. I don't know anyone in town and really can't afford to stay at a motel. I spent all my spare change getting here from my last billet and I won't get my first check from the V.A. until the beginning of the month."

Jordan sighed. "I can't afford to go anywhere either. And I won't get any checks -- my scholarship pays for tuition and, if I stay in the dorm, room and board, but that's it. That's the only reason I'm here."

"Well, I'm little bit better off since I am here by choice Joined the Navy right after high school and missed out on college life so I decided to go for the full experience, at least for the first year."

"Wouldn't that mean joining a frat with your buddies?" She jutted her chin toward the door.

"Buddies? Just met 'em. Recruited them to help me get my bags up here."

"Where the hell were they when I had to drag up all those boxes by myself?"

"From their breath out drinking." He looked the stack up and down. "Were you planning on taking over the whole room?"

She shook her head. "Most of that doesn't need to be unpacked. But, it's all I have to show for the past fifteen years of my life and I can't afford a storage locker."

Dennis shoved his hands in his pockets. "I'm guessing, there's a lot of meaning in those words, but right now you look tuckered out and I could do with a shower and some sleep myself. I've got enough scratch for two tickets to the Brats & Brew fundraiser tomorrow night, care to join me? We can fortify ourselves until the cafeteria opens on Monday."

Jordan smiled and pointed at the cooler stashed under one desk. "And, I spent the last of my spare change on cold cuts and a loaf of bread so if you feed us tomorrow, I can feed us Sunday."

"Deal." Dennis offered his hand again and when his huge palm enfolded her small one, gave it an exaggerated shake."Now, I'm going to avail myself of the facilities, which I figure can't be any worse than I've," he cleared his throat, "enjoyed for the past for eight years. If you want to take advantage of my absence to find something to sleep in besides the all together, it might be a little less embarrassing in the morning."

Jordan blushed. "How did...?"

"The way you're clutching at those blankets."

Jordan pulled them over her head and didn't peak out again until she heard the door open and close.

After endless hours of introductions, mingling with college students who seemed half her age and professors who didn't appear to be much older, and lugging around what seemed like a ream of paper full of repetitious drivel, Jordan had second thoughts about spending the evening with Dennis. But, her grumbling stomach and her overwhelming desire for a beer persuaded her to meet him outside the tent set up in the middle of the quad. They stood in line for paper plates full of sour kraut and baked beans with a single brat in a bun and assurances they could come back for seconds. Dennis found them an empty table in the far corner of the tent and left her there with the food. By the time he returned with two large plastic cups of foaming beer, Jordan had emptied her plate and was eyeing his.

"I take it you were a tad hungry?" Dennis sat down across from her. "Sorry it took so long to get the beer, but that line was longer than the one for chow."

Jordan took a sip. It was cold. It quenched her thirst. Other than that ...

"From your face, I'm guessing your used to better beer?"

Jordan shrugged. "Lived in the Pacific Northwest."

"You're gonna hate the coffee."

She smiled. "I take it you're not as picky?"

"Ma'am, I just spent eight years of my life eating aboard a destroyer. Once you've tasted burned rice, most anything else is edible."

"Why'd you join the Navy?"

"As trite as it sounds, to see the world. Which I did. Plus, when I was eighteen, I didn't know what I wanted to do or be."

"And, now?"

"I want to teach. Preferably science. And, what about you and your stack of boxes?"

Jordan shook her head.

"Did he beat you, cheat on you, or ...?"

She nodded and drained her cup. "Think I'll go get me another brat."

"I'm right behind you." He grinned and grabbed both plates.

She followed him back through the line. By now the crowd had thinned out and they persuaded the servers to give them each two brats. Back at the table, Dennis produced a stack of napkins and they wrapped up one each, tucking them into their coat pockets.

"Breakfast." He winked.

She took a bite out of a brat-filled bun.

Dennis grabbed another napkin and wiped at the juice that trickled from the corner of her mouth. "I don't know how you ended up in the straits that made living in a college dorm your only option, but you can count on me as a friend. Tomorrow, I'll help you come up with a way to store your boxes that won't make your next roomie cringe. But, given that we're probably the two oldest students in the dorm, we should have each other's backs."

She couldn't help smiling at him. But, if he'd spent eight years in the Navy, he was only twenty-six, four years her junior.

"What do you plan to study?"

She shrugged. "Starting from scratch. Never finished high school, just got my GED this summer. Don't have to declare a major until second year, so I'm taking basic classes and exploring."

She sighed. Although he was younger than her, he had a plan. She'd grabbed the scholarship because it offered her an escape. But until she received her awards letter, she'd never even considered attending college. She'd be the first female in her family that did so, not that any of them would ever know about it.

"Well, if I'm frugal, I can probably afford to take you out once or twice a month as long as you're willing to go cheap."

She tilted her head. "Why? If you want the entire experience shouldn't you be dating girls your own age and getting drunk on weekends?"

He laughed. "I've done my share of binge drinking and I can live without the hangovers, thank you. As to women, well, I'd have thought you were," he pulled air quotes, "my own age if you hadn't apparently spent fifteen years in a bad marriage. Besides, most of the females I've met so far are girls, and I find women more appealing."

Jordan bent over her beans, scraping them off her plate with her plastic fork, to avoid looking in his eyes.

He leaned forward and whispered in her ear. "Don't worry. I gave you my word that I'd be the perfect gentleman and I will. Just please promise me you'll let me know if you ever think you might like to be more than friends."

"We should go. Looks like we're the last ones hanging around."

The servers were stacking the steam trays onto carts and rolling the kegs out the door.

Dennis gathered up their garbage. "Must of run out of beer."

⌒ঌ

In the morning, after devouring their purloined brats, Dennis helped Jordan extract the few things she thought she would need from her boxes. She filled one of the two built-in armoires that had drawers on one side and a foot of hanging space on the other. Dennis stashed two each of the remaining boxes on top of the armoires and shoved the other two into the far corners under the desks.

Standing up and brushing off his hands, he said, "That's better."

"Unless, they make me move." Given how far away the showers were, she wondered if the women's rooms were on the other side of the dorm.

"We don't have to tell admin they screwed up." He grinned. "Maybe stay with the known awkward rather than risk getting stuck with total douchebags?"

"As long as I can have the top bunk."

"Whichever you prefer." He bowed from the waist.

"Let's unpack those seabags."

⌒ঌ

As midterms approached, Jordan grew more and more tense. She struggled in all but one of her classes and anything less than a B plus average would cost her the scholarship. She couldn't go back. But, she'd never had a job and didn't know how she would support herself if she got tossed.

She couldn't make sense of half the stuff her teachers said and the textbook wasn't much better. Alone in the room, she crawled under her desk, her arms wrapped around her knees. So many times she'd hidden under the living room table in exactly this position, holding her breath, silently weeping.

Dennis found her there, shaking, tears streaming down her face. He sat cross legged on the floor in front of her desk and opened his arms. Jordan crawled out and he pulled her into his lap, wrapping her gently in his muscled arms, rocking back and forth with her.

"What's wrong, Jordan?"

"Can't go back." She hiccoughed.

"Of course not, you don't have to go back, ever."

"I'll lose my scholarship if I don't make good grades." She sobbed.

"Then, we'll just have to make sure you get good grades. I wish you'd have let me know sooner you were having trouble. Let's get to work. Which is your first midterm?"

"Algebra."

"Easy as pie." He helped her to her feet and sat her down at her desk, pulling his own chair over next to hers.

Three hours later, it started actually making sense and Jordan kissed him on the cheek.

He grinned. "What say we break for dinner and then we can tackle English."

She rolled her eyes. "Don't you need to study?"

He shook his head. "Not really. I saved up and bought myself an e-reader my first year in the Navy and devoured anything and everything I could download onto it, mostly free stuff from Project Gutenberg. So far my classes haven't covered any new ground. If I didn't need a degree to teach, I'd probably abandon ship from sheer boredom."

"I hope you stick it out. You'll make a fabulous teacher." Jordan followed him down the stairs to the cafeteria.

Jordan refreshed the browser over and over again, but the screen didn't change.

"You're going to wear out the refresh button."

She jumped. She hadn't heard Dennis come back into the room.

"Sorry, didn't mean to startle you. Grades have to be posted by tomorrow -- your teachers could be the procrastinating type."

She slumped in her chair.

"C'mon, I've still got some scratch left for this month. Let's splurge on dinner and a movie."

She shook her head and hit the refresh button again, staring at the screen when it finally rewrote to display her grades for the term.

"Congratulations." He sounded very pleased with himself.

Jordan blinked and looked again. Three Bs and an A. All the hours Dennis had invested in helping her study had paid off. Finally believing her own eyes, she jumped up and wrapped her arms around his waist. At first, he kept his hands at his side, but when she didn't release him, he gently rested one arm across her shoulders and stroked her too-thin, too-straight hair with his other hand. Jordan tensed up and he stopped.

"What the hell did that bastard do to you, woman?" He sighed. "You don't have to answer, but if you don't want to talk to me, maybe you should check out the counselors at the student center and see if you could find one you *are* comfortable talking to."

Jordan clung to him, holding him as tightly as she could, pressing her cheek against his firm chest. She trembled and sobbed.

Wrapping his arms around her, Dennis backed up to his bunk and sat down, pulling her onto his lap and cradling her head against his shoulder. Jordan wept, soaking his tee shirt with her tears. When she stopped shaking and her breathing returned to normal, Dennis released her. She tightened her grip, unwilling to leave the comfort he offered. He reacted by holding her in his arms so gently she could push out of them if she wanted to. She didn't want to.

She tilted her head back and looked up into his eyes which ranged from sky blue to sapphire depending on the shirt he wore and the lighting. Now they seemed darker than ever. Jordan put one hand on his cheek and he bent down until his lips were within kissing distance. She could smell Old Spice and peppermint. Lifting her head enough to make contact, she touched her lips to his. He put one hand gently on the back of her neck and opened his mouth slightly.

Intrigued, she extended her tongue and tasted the flavors of mouthwash mixed with coffee. He met the tip of her tongue with his own and they danced between each other's mouths. Jordan's breath came in gasps and she felt flushed, wondering if she should kiss a man if she was coming down with a fever. When she pulled back, a look of disappointment flashed across his features.

"Thanks. I've wanted to do that since the day we met."

Jordan tilted her head.

"No, that's not all I've wanted to do. You're an amazingly beautiful woman and I would very much like to make love to you, have wanted to for a long time now."

Not beautiful, not even pretty. "But?"

"But, do you want to make love to me? Or any man for that matter?"

Jordan swallowed hard. She didn't consider having sex making love and it wasn't something she enjoyed. But, she had to admit Dennis made her feel warm and tingly in a way that she'd never experienced before. And, he had helped her get through the last semester with tutoring, moral support, and date night escapes from dorm food.

She put her arms around his neck and kissed him again. Beneath her rear, she felt the unmistakable hardening and almost pulled away. But, she had no other way to repay him for everything he had done for her. At least she knew he wouldn't hurt her.

Dennis released her lips and looked into her eyes. "Are you sure?"

Part of her wanted to scream, "No!" to push him away, crawl up into her bunk and pull the covers over her head. But she nodded and nuzzled his neck with her nose.

"You don't know how long I've wished, hoped, you would feel comfortable enough with me to say yes. I've fallen in love with you, Jordan and I want you more than I've ever wanted any woman I've known. But, if you change your mind, if it's too much, just say no and I'll stop."

Jordan just stared at him. Of course men reached a point where they no longer could control themselves, but it was a nice thought.

Dennis ran his knuckle along her cheek and dragged his finger down to the neck of her oversized tee shirt. "May I take this off?"

She sucked in her breath. Once she took off her clothes, no matter what he said, they would pass the point of no return. Jordan closed her eyes and moved her head up and down just an inch.

Dennis picked up the bottom of the shirt and lifted it up until he was stopped by her arms clamped to her sides. Would he still be interested when he saw how flat chested she was? *Never stopped* .... She chased the thought away and lifted her arms so he could pull the shirt over her head, tossing it up onto the top bunk. "Beautiful." He leaned down, his breath hot against her chest, and inhaled.

Jordan figured he was just saying that to be nice. His lips moved to the hollow at the base of her neck and then back down to tease the tops of her breasts, covering them with light, feathery kisses. She gasped, her breathing ragged. Dennis' fingers had found the clasp of her bra. "May I?"

His voice startled her. He'd already taken off her shirt?

Did he intend to consult her before he removed every piece of clothing? "Yes," she whispered.

The bra joined her shirt and Dennis cupped one breast in his hand while licking his way down to the nipple of the other. Jordan moaned. Her breasts had been pawed, bitten, and bruised but never licked. She wiggled, sensations she'd never experienced coursing through her. Dennis sucked one nipple gently and she felt her cotton panties growing damp. Had she peed on herself? And, on Dennis? She debated stopping him so she could go to the washroom, but it was so far away.

His fingers had found their way to the button of her jeans and he released her nipple just long enough to repeat: "May I?"

Jordan didn't want him to discover she'd wet herself, but she didn't want to stop him, either.

"'kay."

He unfastened her jeans and worked one finger between her legs. She pressed her thighs together.

He lifted his head. "Do you want me to stop?"

Jordan tried to catch her breath and figure out how to answer his question. If it weren't for the embarrassingly wet panties ...

"I think I need to go to the bathroom."

"Jordan, have you ever enjoyed sex?"

She just stared at him. What was there to enjoy? And what did that have to do with the tightness in her groin and her damp underwear?

"What you're feeling may not be a need to pee." He cupped a breast in each hand, gently tweaking her nipples with his thumbs. "The human female was designed to get a great deal of pleasure from intercourse, but requires certain kinds of stimulation to get there. If your husband?" He tilted his head to one side and when she didn't respond he continued, "just used your body to satisfy himself, you may not have experienced any pleasure before. Please, let me show you how lovely it can be."

She rolled her eyes but relaxed her thighs. He returned his

mouth to her nipple, his free hand floated down her belly, and his finger found it's way between her legs to the source of all her pain and suffering. Jordan closed her eyes and cringed, but a moment later, she gasped and grabbed his shoulders. He didn't go all the way in, just rubbed the tip of one finger near the top of her cleft. She squirmed. She both wanted to get free of his finger and didn't want him to stop. The lower half of her body tensed and then she shook. Desperately, she tried to regain control, but her body wouldn't respond. Gripping Dennis' shoulders, she screamed. Finally, she collapsed against his chest gasping for breath. He wrapped his arms around her until she stopped shaking.

"What did you do to me?"

He chuckled. "I'm guessing from your reaction I just had the honor of giving you your first orgasm."

Jordan tried to lift her head, but it ended up falling backwards. Dennis put his hand behind her neck and grinned. He seemed almost as proud of himself as when he'd seen her grades.

He leaned down and whispered in her ear. "Now that we've got you all wet and ready, would you like to try more?"

Unsure her body was capable of more, unwilling to stop, she managed to nod. Dennis pulled the blankets back on his bed and sat her down on the sheets. He stripped off her pants, underwear, and flipflops then rose and removed his own clothing. She had to admire his muscular body, but the part jutting out at her face was bigger than she had ever seen. She sighed and opened her mouth.

"Do you want to do that or do you think it's required?"

She pressed her lips together and could feel her chin trembling.

"Don't worry. It's not required. I hope one day you'll want to give me a blow job, but I don't want you to ever feel obligated to do so." Dennis extracted a condom from his desk drawer, tore open the packet, and slipped it on. He sat down next to her, one arm over her shoulder, the fingers of his other hand caressing her thighs. "I'm going to lay on my back. You can straddle me. That way you're in complete control. You can jump off and get into your own bed anytime you want to, although if you do that at this point I hope you won't be upset if I jack off down here."

He stretched out in the middle of his bed, leaving her perched on the edge of his bunk. She didn't want to stop, but somehow knowing she could at any time erased the tension that had built between her shoulder blades. Jordan turned and balanced on her knees on the edge of the bunk. Dennis held out his hands, and she gripped them while she threw one leg over his hips. When she put her hands down on either side of his neck, he caressed her breasts.

She wasn't quite sure what do next and gave him a quizzical look. He put his hands on her hips and guided her lower in the bunk until she was positioned over his sheathed cock. With one hand, he guided it to her entrance. "Whenever you're ready, love."

Jordan blinked rapidly. He didn't move. She lowered her hips just enough to feel the tip against her hole. It felt good. It had never felt good, before. She eased down his length and moaned. It felt really good. Dennis fondled a breast with one hand, and moved his thumb back into the position his finger had found before. She gasped. Of their own volition, her hips moved up and down and she slid along the length of his cock. His thumb pressed upwards and her eyes rolled back in her head.

She started shaking again and fell forward onto his chest, unable to budge. Dennis took over the movement and she clung to him, waves of ecstacy rolling over her again and again. Then he groaned and stopped. She could feel his heart beating against her chest. They were both breathing hard. Dennis wrapped his arms around her back and held her close. She rested her cheek against his shoulder. He softened and slipped out and for the first time she wished there was more.

"Don't worry, sweetheart. I'm not a teenager anymore,

but give me a little bit to rest and I can get that up again for you."

Jordan grinned. She finally knew what she wanted to study in school. There had to be a program that would train her to teach other survivors that sex could feel good and not all men were abusers. Nuzzling Dennis' neck, she fell asleep in his arms.

Gordon

By I.G. Frederick

"Oh my word! Gordon!" Lenore clapped her hand over her mouth and blushed. She hoped the man with muscular shoulders hidden under a leather jacket, thick blond hair with the signature cowlick in front, and green eyes that reminded her of jade didn't hear her. But, he stopped short of the barista and looked in her direction.

His smile would have set one of her characters all a flutter. "Were you speaking to me?"

She tried to shake her head, but nodded instead.

"My name's not Gordon. Are you confusing me with someone else?" He faced the counter just long enough to place an order and hand over his credit card.

When he returned his attention to her, Lenore managed to shake her head from side to side. Slowly she lowered her hand from her mouth. "You're a model."

"Yes. You've seen my work?" He grinned like an overgrown teen.

Unable to form words, Lenore minimized her word pro-

17

cessor and turned her laptop so he could see the wallpaper showing her latest release.

He laughed, throwing his head back. "I take it that's Gordon?" He pointed at the half naked man embracing a barely clothed woman on the book cover.

She nodded.

"God that woman was a bitch. Worst. Shoot. Ever. Swore from then on, I work alone. I hope her character in," he peered at the screen, *Summer to Remember* is nicer."

Lenore bit her lip to avoid bursting into tears. Serena was absolutely her favorite female character. Stumbling across their series on a stock photo site had inspired Lenore to create five books featuring Serena and Gordon.

"I didn't mean to upset you." He looked at her screen again. "Crap, are you Lillian Lyris?"

"One of my pen names." She realized those were the most words she'd managed to string together since she'd spotted him entering her Friday coffee shop. But the man took her breath away just by standing across the table from her.

"I suppose the bitch is your heroine?"

She looked at her hands, folded in her lap to hide her unpolished, bitten-to-the-quick nails. "I didn't know."

The barista called out, "Rich," and he retrieved his coffee. Lenore sighed, relief mixed with regret, and returned her screen to the word processor. Before she could type a full sentence, Rich sat down across from her.

"So, tell me more about Gordon." He took a sip from a giant cup of coffee, distorting the heart painted in foam across the top.

She felt her cheeks grow warm and shrugged. "Typical romance hero, handsome, rugged, wary of commitment." The series wasn't just about romance, but it definitely qualified as "chick lit," so she didn't figure Rich would want more details.

"I'm intrigued." He grinned. "Not something I'd ordinarily choose, but how can I not read a book I'm the hero in?"

Lenore extracted a bookmark from her laptop case and handed it to him. "Not exactly the hero. Just a character inspired by your photographs."

"How many books have you published?"

"*Summer to Remember* is my twenty-sixth."

"Wow!" He put his elbows on the table and leaned forward. "You've written twenty-six novels? How long did that take? When did you start, when you were five?"

She tilted her head, wondering whether he was flirting or just awed by being on a book cover. Surely if he modeled professionally it wasn't a big deal.

"I've written thirty novels. I started writing full time six years ago."

"You write five novels a year? How?"

"One sentence at a time."

He grinned. "You said Lillian Lyris was *one* of your pen names. How many do you have?"

"Three. One I use for romances, one for mysteries, and Lyris for what you'd probably call chick lit."

"And how did I end up on the cover of *Summer to Remember*?"

"I purchased all five photos from your *worst shoot ever* and am writing an entire series with Gordon and Serena."

"Oh, you're self published?" The excitement in his green eyes faded and he emptied his cup.

Lenore debated letting him go so she could get back to work. But, she hated disdain from people who knew nothing about the business. "I sold my fifth novel to a New York publisher, but after sixteen books. I turned them down because I can make more money on my own."

He cocked his head. "Really? Do you write full time?"

She nodded.

"You can make a living? I thought all writers were poor starving artists?"

"That seems to be the big publishers' goal. But, my writing's paid the bills for the past five years." Of course the bills were much smaller now that she only had to support herself. "Speaking of which, I probably should get back to it." She held out her hand. "Nice meeting you, Rich."

He turned her hand and pressed his lips to her fingers, looking down at her with a twinkle in his eyes. She had to grip the table with her other hand to keep from shuddering or worse batting her eyelashes.

"Don't suppose you'd go out with me? Love to hear more about your work."

She pulled her hand back from the tingling sensation of his touch, torn between her attraction and the banality of his questions. "Do you like explaining how to get into the modeling business?"

He laughed. "Point taken. Although that's just a sideline. My day job is in social services. Tell you what, if you let me take you to dinner, I promise not to ask you about writing or bore you with the details of my job."

Lenore frowned. Picking a social worker's brain made the prospect of going out with Rich more appealing not less. *Only a writer would prefer to date someone who can talk about helping people rather than a hunky model.* He *was* incredibly handsome. Which made her wonder why he asked. The sedentary lifestyle of a writer had added pounds to an already curvy figure, she wore no makeup, and she was dressed for comfort, including faded sweat pants and an oversized sweat shirt. "Why?"

He shrugged. "Why not? You're cute, you think I'm a hunk, and you have an interesting career."

The last male who called her cute was her high school sweetheart. She looked at the clock on computer screen. *Seriously behind.* "Maybe next week."

"You'll call?" He slipped her a business card.

"Sure." Lenore typed the next sentence in her novel.

The white card with black, block letters sat on the table

next to her front door until Monday when Cathy reminded her about the gala on Thursday. Lenore studied the card before dialing.

"Hi, Rich, this is Lenore. We met at the Hazel Room last week."

"The author? I'm so glad you called. I finished *Enchanted Spring* Saturday and I'm halfway through *Summer to Remember*. Loving them both. When's the next one coming out?"

She pressed the mute button while she giggled. Even if he was just trying to make points, it was still a nice gesture. "I'll finish writing by the end of next week. It usually takes a couple of months for proof reading, cover design, and interior layout. Probably end of January, beginning of February."

"I can hardly wait. I read the entire first book in one day. But, I decided to slow down and savor *Summer to Remember* 'cause I wasn't sure how long I'd have to wait for the sequel."

She still couldn't tell if he was jerking her chain. "Listen, I was wondering if you were free Thursday. I have to go to a fundraiser and I don't have an escort."

"I'm not free, but I don't have a date. Are you talking about the gala? I'd be delighted to escort you."

Lenore blinked several times. At least she wouldn't have to spring for a second ticket. "Great. Do you want to just meet there?"

"Hoping you'd let me buy you dinner, first. Gala food's fancy but hardly filling."

Does this guy have a BBW fetish? "I guess. Where?"

"How about Ringside Fishhouse at six?"

How could she resist? "Okay."

During dinner, Rich kept his promise and they avoided all work-related subjects. They discovered they enjoyed similar books, movies, and music and both loved to hike trails along the central coast.

He looked even more attractive in a black tux that fit so well she wondered if he actually owned it. Although she'd planned on wearing her standard velvet two piece, Lenore had splurged on a blue dress that emphasized her cleavage and disguised her chunky waist and too-large hips with layers of chiffon.

"How is it that a lovely lady such as yourself is still single?"

She frowned. "Divorced. He wanted to know when I'd stop pretending to be an author and get a *real* job." She pulled air quotes. "Ironically, last year I earned more than when I was a store manager and my feet don't hurt every night." She tilted her head. "What about you?"

"Social services pays even less than retail and most women still expect a man to bring home a big check."

"Even in Portland? Maybe you've just dated the wrong women?"

"Or maybe I was just biding time until you found my pictures?" He winked and handed a credit card to the waiter.

Walking the three blocks to the ballroom, Lenore realized she was already tipsy and she'd only drunk one glass of wine with dinner. She resisted reaching for Rich's hand, suspecting her reaction to his touch would only increase her intoxication. After they handed over their tickets, Rich checked their wet coats. Moments later Lenore had a glass of champagne in her hands and friends flocking around her waiting for her to introduce them to Rich. They pretended they were interested in seeing her and they all asked about her novel. But, she watched them bat their eyelashes, plump their lips, and stand as close to him as they could.

To her surprise, Rich was impeccably polite, but ignored their flirtations. *Of course, he's probably used to women throwing themselves at him.* She still didn't understand his interest in her, although she couldn't help enjoying the obvious envy of every woman in the room. After greeting her friends and colleagues and introducing her to his, Rich begged her to join him on the dance floor.

"I'm not much of a dancer, maybe you should ask some-one else."

"Why in the world would I want to dance with anyone besides my date?" He tugged her by the hand until she followed him to the open area in front of the six-piece band alternating between toe-tapping tunes and slow sultry songs. Rich took her left hand in his right, put his other hand on her right shoulder, and pulled her close enough so her breasts grazed his chest. "Just follow my lead," he whispered.

He twirled her around the dance area, leading her through movements that left her breathless. She quickly figured out how to hold her arms and torso so her feet followed his steps precisely, and only tromped on his toes once. After their third dance, the band took a break and Rich leaned down, grazing her lips with his. If he hadn't steadied her with a hand on the small of her back, she would have lost her balance.

He led her to one of the tables surrounding the dance area and left her trying to catch her breath.

"Your new beau is a divine dancer, I do hope you're going to share."

Lenore looked up to see Sheila who she only knew casually from Sisters in Crime. A tall, stunning, blonde, she wore a painted on black sequined gown and six-inch, fuck-me pumps.

"You'll have to ask him." *Oh, well, it was fun while it lasted.*

"Ask me what?" Rich set a plate in front of her loaded with goodies from the buffet table and sat down next to her with an equally full plate.

She stabbed a stuffed mushroom with the fork. By now four women she knew surrounded her and Rich.

"I'm Sheila." The blonde handed Rich her hand, palm down.

He turned it and gave it a shake.

"I was just telling Lenore that you dance divinely and I hoped she wouldn't be selfish and keep you all to yourself."

"Thanks, but I'm afraid my dance card's full, ladies."

Lenore almost choked on the stuffed date she had popped into her mouth. The flavors of butter, blue cheese, and dried fruit assaulted her senses.

"You okay, Sweetie?" Rich waved at a waiter passing on the opposite side of the table and handed Lenore one of the two glasses of champagne the man set down in front of them.

Sweetie?!?! Lenore sipped enough of the bubbly to clear her throat, leaned over and whispered in Rich's ear. "I don't mind, really."

He gave her a stern look. "Yes, you do."

Lenore popped a croquette into her mouth, but was too distracted to even identify the filling.

Rich leaned over and whispered in her ear. "Besides, if someone does me the honor of asking me to be her escort, it'd be rude to dance with anyone else." He touched the tip of his tongue to her earlobe and Lenore almost slid off her chair.

"I guess we'd better leave these two lovebirds alone." Sheila spun around and minced away, swaying her hips as if to show Rich what he was missing. The others drifted toward other tables when Rich ignored them.

"Is the blonde always such a nuisance?"

Lenore shrugged her shoulders. "Barely know her. She belongs to one of my writing groups."

"Reminds me of the bitch. I will say, I like Serena a lot more than either of them. I was hoping she might be semi-autobiographical."

The heat traveled from Lenore's cheeks all the way down to her chest. She emptied her champagne glass. "Not really. I would make a horribly boring novel."

"Don't be ridiculous. I find you fascinating."

Lenore stared at him. She could see nothing in his face to indicate anything but sincerity.

"Why don't you finish fueling up so we can dance some more." He nodded toward the stage where the players were picking up their instruments.

If this guy sticks around, I'm going to have to take lessons.

Lenore emptied her plate and Rich rose to his feet offering her his hand. When she placed her palm against his, trying to ignore the electric charges stabbing through her, he pulled her into his arms and danced away with her.

They only sat down when the band stopped playing. Lenore was almost grateful when the players packed up their instruments. While they waited for their coats, Rich tried to persuade Lenore to go to breakfast with him.

She shook her head. "I'm exhausted, my feet are killing me, and," she checked the time on her cell, "It's way too late for me -- I start writing at nine." She noted three texts from friends, all variations of "Who's that hunk you're with?"

"You can't take a morning off?"

"Not and meet my deadlines." She winked. "You're not the only one waiting for *Autumn Ardor*. Besides, don't you have to work?"

He smiled. "I'm on call one weekend a month, so I get every other Friday off." He held her coat out for her to slip her arms into. "What about tomorrow night?"

Lenore fumbled with her buttons. *What is this guy after?* "Look, Rich, I had a really fabulous time tonight, but ..."

"I did, too. I really like you Lenore. I want to get to know you better." They paused near the entrance, hesitating before stepping back out into the cold rain. He leaned down and whispered in her ear, his breath hot on the sensitive skin of her neck. "Much, much better." He dragged his tongue from the base of her neck to the back of her ear.

Lenore tried to push him away, but her hands wouldn't rise, her arms hung by her side, useless tubes of jelly.

Rich nibbled on her ear lobe. Lenore couldn't catch her breath.

"If you'd let me, I'd take you home and ravish you right now. Hell, I'd take you over to the Paramount and get a room." He blew into her ear and Lenore had to lean against the wall to keep her feet.

Well, now she knew what he wanted, although she

couldn't imagine why. The question was what was she going to do about it? She turned her head toward him and his lips collided with hers sending her senses reeling. He wrapped his muscled arms around her, holding her against his chest, the only thing keeping her from falling over.

They were both breathing heavily when he finally released her lips and licked his way back to her ear. "We should go somewhere a bit more private. Paramount, my place, or yours?"

The dizziness that overwhelmed her had nothing to do with champagne. She'd finished her last glass two hours ago. Somehow her arms had found their way around Rich's neck and she clung to him.

"Just nod once for a hotel, twice for my place by Lloyd Center, or three times for your place.

She didn't imagine a social worker could afford a downtown hotel room, especially not after a gala ticket and an expensive dinner. Her place was further away and she'd left dishes in the sink, the bed unmade, and dirty clothes on the bedroom floor. She nodded twice.

"Can you make it to the Max, or should I call a cab?"

She released his neck and pushed herself away from the wall, then grabbed his arm when she realized she could no longer balance on heels. Rich held her with one arm while extracting his cell from his shirt pocket. Minutes later, he handed her into the back of a Radio Cab.

They were dropped off in front of a two-story brick building. Rich wrapped his arm around her back and guided her halfway down a corridor. After he unlocked his door and flipped a light switch, he scooped her up into his arms and carried her into a sparsely furnished living room, kicking the door closed behind them. A black leather sofa along the wall faced a small round oak table with two chairs under the window. He carried her past an immaculate, u-shaped kitchen into a bedroom which contained only a king-sized bed, an oak chest of drawers, and a miniature version of the drawers next to the bed. A brass lamp sat on top of the nightstand, the bed was covered in a black comforter, and nothing was on he wooden floor, not even a rug.

Rich set her on her feet and helped her out of her coat. He took it and his own out of the room and returned before Lenore could question why she was in a stranger's bedroom. Putting one hand on either side of her face, he leaned down and kissed her. At first, his lips only pressed against hers. But, when she opened them, he plunged his tongue between her teeth and she sucked on it greedily.

His kiss sent shock waves through her entire body and she didn't even realize he had stripped off their clothing until he clasped his naked chest against her exposed breasts. His hands grasped her ass cheeks, holding her tight against his muscled legs and the erection that pressed into her belly. Rich didn't seem to care how big her ass was or that her belly protruded and her thighs met even when her feet were apart.

His lips moved from her mouth down her neck. He lifted one tit off her chest and sucked on her nipple until she couldn't keep her feet. When she fell backward, Rich caught her, eased her onto the bed, and stretched out beside her. The comforter had been tossed aside and cool black linen sheets welcomed her flushed skin. Rich's hands caressing her thighs, fondling her breasts, stroking her arms sent heat radiating through her until even the sheets were warm.

A finger found its way into her folds and Lenore gasped.

She was vaguely aware of a drawer opening and a condom package ripping. Rich pulled her on top of him. Straddling his hips, she stared at the amazing hunk of man flesh beneath her. He had his hands on her tits, gently squeezing them, his eyes practically rolled back in his head, his lips parted. Sliding herself down onto his sheathed cock, she moaned. Rich put one hand on her ass, stroking her inflamed skin. He let her set the pace while caressing her everywhere. Placing her hands on either side of his face, she leaned forward and kissed him. He tangled his fingers in her hair, pushing his hips up so his pubes pressed against her clit.

Unable to support her weight, Lenore collapsed. Afraid she would crush him, she aimed to land on her side next to him. Rich rolled with her until she was flat on her back and he knelt between her thunder thighs. He plunged into her, his mouth covering hers, their tongues dancing, until Lenore cried out. The trembling started in her clit, but Rich moved faster and harder until her whole body shook beneath him.

She was still coming when he cried out and then lay still. He covered her face with kisses and then eased onto his side, one arm under her neck, the other beneath her breasts, and his leg across her thighs. Still gasping for breath, Lenore put her hand on his arm. He laced their fingers together, without slackening his hug.

"Will you spend the night with me?" He nuzzled her neck. "It would be wonderful to wake up with you in my arms so I could make love to you again and then fix you breakfast. I promise I'll take you home in time to get to work."

Lenore couldn't keep her eyes open and had no idea how she would stay awake long enough to get dressed and find her way home. She turned her head so she faced Rich. She wanted to run her fingers through his thick blond hair and pull his cowlick back into place, but didn't have the strength. When she nodded, he grinned and kissed her on the forehead.

"Good night, my love. Sleep well."

Love? Wow, this guy doesn't waste any time. Lenore didn't know about love, but the sex was hot, she enjoyed Rich's company, and all her friends were jealous. She closed her eyes and succumbed to the delicious lethargy creeping up from her toes.

Spa Date

By I.G. Frederick

"But, Samantha," Julia whined. She knew Sam hated her full name and only used it when she wanted to annoy her friend. "It'll be fun."

Sam produced her best macho glare, arms across her chest, chin lowered, eyebrows pulled together.

"Please?" Almost a head shorter than Sam, Julia tilted her neck and batted her eyelashes. "Everyone else in my wedding party will be there."

"Everyone else in your wedding party is as girly and straight as you." Sam preferred femme girls, but Julia was just too much of a prima donna. They had little in common other than growing up next door to each other -- sharing secrets, sleepovers, homework, and sexual discoveries.

"Come, on, Sam. You don't have to get any polish. They can trim your nails as short as you like. Tell me you wouldn't like to have a hot Asian babe massaging lotion into your feet and rubbing oil onto your fingers?"

Sam raised one eyebrow over the other. “Hot Asian babes? My type or are they all straight?”

Julia shrugged. “How would I know? It’s not like we talk about our sex lives while I have my nails done. But, do you really care, when you can get away with staring down her cleavage for an hour?”

Sam sighed. Accepting Julia’s invitation to be her maid of honor had been a difficult decision and she agreed only as long as she was referred to as “best woman” and could wear a tux like the groomsmen. When she discovered she was expected to throw Julia a wedding shower and organize a bachelorette party, she almost backed out.

Even if Julia wasn’t her type, the woman knew how to push all Sam’s buttons. Unbeknownst to her friends, Julia planned the entire shower herself so Sam only had to email the invitations, written by Julia, and collect the responses. And Julia came up with the idea of a spa date instead of a bachelorette party which would have been fine if she didn’t insist Sam go along.

“No amount of exposed tittie is going to make it worth putting up with the stench of nail polish and smelly lotions.”

“But, this place doesn’t stink, I promise. They use fragrance-free lotions and environmentally friendly nail polish.” Julia pulled the neck of her t-shirt down revealing plump, creamy breasts. “And they all wear tight black outfits with lots of exposed cleavage.”

Sam let her breath out and scowled. “If I can’t breathe I’m walking out.”

Julia grinned.

Julia and her bridesmaids wore frilly summer dresses with plunging necklines. Sam had on straight-legged black jeans, knee-high leather boots, and a black t-shirt. One by one, tiny Asian women wearing tight black pants and frilly black blouses with black hair tied back in pony tails or braids that reached their pert little asses came out to escort the bridal party back into the bowels of the torture chamber.

A woman wearing rectangular dark red glasses, who had lustrous, auburn-dyed hair curling around her face and caressing her shoulders, emerged and called out, "Mr. Sam?"

Sam chuckled and stepped forward. "I'm Sam."

The woman's face lit up and she bowed. "Most pleased to meet you Ms. Sam. I am Yen Lee. Please to follow me."

Sam watched the woman's tight, round globes undulate toward the back and strode after her. The bridesmaids and Julia giggled and gossiped, each ensconced in a large, leather recliner, their feet in swirling tubs of water.

Yen led Sam to a display of nail polish in every color imaginable. "You pick a color, yes?"

Sam shook her head. "No thanks. No polish."

"Yes, Ma'am. No polish." Yen smiled. "This way, if you please."

The girls had taken all the stations along the wall. Yen bowed before a leather recliner with its back to the window looking out over the shopping mall. After Sam sat, Yen carried over a foot bath full of water and set it on the floor in front of the chair. Sam stuck out one foot. Yen turned her back and grabbed hold of Sam's boot. Sam had to resist an urge to place the other heel against Yen's most attractive ass. The girl quickly pulled off both boots, removed Sam's socks, stuffed them inside, and pushed the legs of her jeans as high on her calves as they would go.

Sam lifted her legs and Yen slid the foot bath underneath, waving her hand until Sam lowered her feet into the warm water. Yen flipped a switch and the water swirled around Sam's ankles. She wriggled her toes and leaned back. Reluctant to admit she was enjoying herself, Sam studied the other spa techs. All of them were pretty, but they also looked as if they'd just stepped off the boat. Ironically, none of them wore colored nail polish or face paint, unlike Yen's bright red nails and artfully applied eye make-up.

The woman who sat behind the reception desk when they entered the spa appeared with a tray of cookies and a stack of paper plates. Sam took two, but turned down the woman's offer of herbal tea. She bit back a complaint that coffee wasn't an option.

One by one, the techs laid towels across small, low tables, and positioned them above the edge of the foot baths. They extracted left feet from the water. The girls pretty much ignored the women working on their feet, continuing their rating of the anatomical attributes of various males of their acquaintance.

When Yen dried the water from her left foot, Sam found it easy to tune out the rest of the bridal party's trivial tittering. Yen unwrapped some metal tools and used one to push back the cuticles on Sam's toes then another to snip off bits of dead skin and trim her nails. Then she buffed Sam's nails until they gleamed without polish before easing her foot back into the water and repeating her ministrations with the right foot.

Switching back to Sam's left foot, Yen dried it off again and her strong hands kneaded the heel and ball, rubbing in lotion and sending tingly tension toward Sam's clit. Looking down Yen's blouse, Sam saw a hint of red lace on Yen's bra. Yen caught her eye and slowly dragged her tongue from one side of her mouth to the other.

Sam growled softly and imagined Yen wearing only the bra and lace panties while massaging her feet.

Yen lowered her eyes, although she kept her tongue visible, peeking out between her painted lips. Sam couldn't help wondering how Yen's tongue would feel on her clit. When Yen massaged lotion into her right foot, Sam ran her left big toe along the edge of Yen's blouse from her collarbone to the button below her delectable cleavage. Yen leaned forward and brought her elbows to her side, capturing Sam's toe between her breasts. Both women inhaled sharply.

One of the other techs minced over and pulled open a drawer in a white chest next to Sam's seat. Yen drew back just enough to release Sam's toe without pausing in her attention to her other foot. She covered both Sam's feet with a hot towel, drew a higher, narrow table over Sam's lap, and draped Sam's arms over a towel-covered, long, rounded pillow. She covered them with another hot, moist towel.

Sam glanced up long enough to see the other girls sitting with foam separating their toes, nails polished in colors ranging from deep red to Julia's bright pink. At least the bride had been right about one thing, the place didn't stink. Sam returned her attention to Yen who rubbed heat into Sam's fingers and hand with the hot towel. Leaning back in the chair, Sam took a deep breath and let it out in one long exhale. She watched Yen wield her tools again.

When Sam's fingernails gleamed, Yen again grabbed the lotion bottle. This time she pursed her lips in a way that made Sam long to stick her fingers in Yen's mouth. She leaned forward, her lips next to Yen's ear. "You *are* planning to give me your phone number?"

Yen batted her eye lashes. "If Ma'am wishes."

"I prefer Sir."

Yen grinned. "Yes, Sir." She left Sam's arms covered and disappeared toward the front. The other girls held their fingers inside black boxes. Yen returned and handed Sam a card. "If Sir would be so kind to ask for Yen again when she returns."

Sam turned the card over. A telephone number was handwritten on the back. Sam smiled and stuck the card in her shirt pocket.

Yen pulled Sam's socks from her boots, shook them out, and drew them onto her feet. She eased the footbath to one side and held Sam's boots for her to step into. When Sam rose to her feet, Yen stayed in her chair. She bowed her head and placed the back of her hands on her thighs, her palms open.

Sam had to restrain her desire to grab her hair and kiss

her in front of the rest of the bridal party. Instead, she stuck a twenty in between Yen's delectable breasts. "What time do you get off?" she whispered.

"Store closes at nine, Sir. I usually can leave by nine thirty."

Sam had to lean down to hear her words."I'll be out front. Look for a red Ford Ranger."

"Yes, Sir. Thank you, Sir."

As the bridesmaids drifted toward the exit, Julie grabbed Sam's arms. "I see you found something you like."

Sam just grinned.

"Let me know if I should change your status from single to bringing a guest."

Sam cocked her head to one side. "Was this a setup?"

Julie grinned. "Let's just say I suspected Yen might be your type and suggested she be your tech. Glad I was right." Her smile disappeared. "Besides, I was the one who introduced you to Celeste. Maybe this time ..."

Sam put an arm over her friend's shoulder and gave her a hug. As annoying as Julie could be at times, she wanted very much for Sam to find someone who would make her happy.

CS

One by one the lights inside the spa blinked out and the technicians emerged from the entrance, giggling and chittering in what sounded like Vietnamese. Yen moved around the group and headed straight for Sam's truck. "Good evening, Sir."

"Hungry?"

"Yes, Sir. Thank you, Sir."

"Hop in."

Sam started the truck and put it in gear as soon as Yen buckled her seatbelt. "Pizza okay?"

"I love pizza with almost anything except anchovies."

Stopped at the entrance to the parking lot, waiting for

traffic to clear, Sam turned and looked Yen up and down, making sure the same woman who had lavished attention on her toes had climbed into her truck."

Yen grinned. "Accent's fake. Otherwise customers just assume I'm uppity and ask for one of the other girls."

Sam grinned back. "I wondered. Your hair color, nail polish, your display of protocols?"

"BDSM isn't unknown in Asia. But, I was born in Chicago. As to protocols, I've been in the lifestyle since my first year of college."

"What did you study?" Sam turned the truck into the parking lot of a strip mall, dark except for the neon glow above the entrance to *Pizza & Pints*.

"I have a Master's in Computer Science." Yen jumped out of the truck as soon as Sam put it in park and dashed around to open Sam's door.

Sam turned in her seat, but instead of jumping down snagged one boot behind Yen's back and pulled her in between her legs. She finally succumbed to her urge to grab Yen's long hair. Running her fingers from Yen's temple to the back of her neck, Sam tightened her grip and pulled her head back. Yen's eyes fluttered closed and she let Sam draw her into her arms. When Sam pressed her mouth against Yen's soft lips, she parted them and welcomed the onslaught of Sam's tongue. Their breath had turned raspy when Sam released Yen and slid down from her seat, caressing Yen's body with her own, enjoying the feel of the shorter woman's plump breasts below her own small ones.

Sam put one arm behind Yen's waist and guided her toward the entrance, kicking the truck door behind her and activating the lock while stuffing her keys into her jeans pocket. Inside, only a few tables were occupied and Sam led Yen to a corner booth in the back, waving to Nicoli so he would know it was occupied.

When Yen slid in along the back wall, Sam joined her on the same side of the table. She rested a hand on Yen's thigh while Nicoli set menus, glasses of ice water, white plates, and tableware wrapped in paper napkins on the checkered red tablecloth in front of them.

"Beer?"

"You still have Black Porter?"

Nicoli nodded.

"Bring me a pint."

"And for your date?"

"An IPA if you have one on tap, please," Yen said.

"We have three ..."

Sam interrupted. "She'll have the Pyramid."

"But, just a glass, please."

"Yes, Ma'am." Nicoli disappeared returning minutes later with a dark pint and a glass of pale ale.

"You're usual pizza, Ma'am?"

"Sure." Sam took a swig of her rich, smooth and creamy malt. She smiled at Yen who took a dainty sip from her glass. "Promise, no anchovies."

Yen batted her lashes. "May I ask what your usual is?"

Sam chuckled. "Meat lover's special -- pepperoni, Canadian bacon, meatballs, salami, and Italian sausage."

Yen licked her lips. "Yum."

Unable to resist, Sam leaned over and sucked Yen's tongue into her mouth. It tasted of hops. With one hand at the base of Yen's neck, Sam pressed their lips together and her other hand glided up Yen's thigh to her tiny waist and glorious tit. The nipple sprang to attention against Sam's palm and the pace of Yen's breathing doubled.

With a sigh, Sam released her lips and her breast. The booth wasn't that private.

"Tell me why someone with a Master's in Computer Science is working as a nail tech?"

"Pays better than unemployment." Yen took another sip of her beer. "I worked my way through college in a salon, and when I got laid off from my job at I-Dek, I realized I could make more in tips than I could get from the state. I send out probably a dozen resumes a week, but I've only had three interviews in six months and the minute they discover I'm female..." She shrugged.

"Might be able to help you with that. I freelance, but I'm getting more work than I can manage. I could probably throw you some subcontracting gigs. I've never met most of my clients and we communicate via e-mail and IM -- they don't know I'm female." Sam pulled her black metal business card case from her jeans pocket and extracted a card. "Send me your resume."

Yen tucked the card into her cleavage. "Thank you, Ma'am. But should we be mixing business and pleasure?"

"Why not?" Sam leaned over and drew her tongue along the length of Yen's neck, tasting orange blossoms in her perfume. Yen gasped.

Sam put her lips to Yen's ear. "Tell me, pretty one have you ever been owned?"

"Collared once. But, none of the women I dated earned my full submission."

"How long were you collared?"

"Eighteen months." She frowned. "The relationship never developed into the dynamic I crave. When I lost my job, I had to choose between moving in with her or moving back home. I chose the latter. My parents may be old school, but I always know where I stand with them."

Sam nibbled on Yen's earlobe. "I promise, I'm always very clear, blunt really, about my expectations. I'm a big believer in communication. When in doubt, I always choose more."

"You don't strike me as someone who's often in doubt." Yen dragged her tongue along Sam's jaw to her ear. "But, I also believe too much communication is much better than too little." Her hot breath burned Sam's skin.

At that moment, Nicoli placed their pie in the middle of the table. Torn between the hunger in her belly and the ache between her legs, Sam almost asked him to box it to go. But, she heard Yen's stomach rumble and realized the girl probably hadn't eaten in hours.

Yen eased a slice onto Sam's plate and put her hands in her lap. Sam cut off the tip of her piece with a knife, picked it up with her fork, and blew on it. She nodded toward the pie. "Enjoy."

"Thank you, Sir." Yen pulled a piece onto her own plate and nibbled at it. "What about you, Sir? Have you owned a slave?"

Sam scowled. "For two years. Turns out she was just using me to train her because the male Dom she wanted wouldn't accept a female with no experience. Figured he'd be less resistant to her advances if she was wearing a woman's collar rather than a man's. Didn't give a shit about what her collar might mean to me."

Yen set her fork down and put her hands in her lap. "If you don't mind me saying so, Sir, I take acceptance of a collar very seriously. Now, I wouldn't even consider wearing one if I didn't believe the woman offering it was someone I could devote my life to serving, someone I would want to marry." She shrugged. "I've learned my lesson, the hard way, about jumping in too quickly and would want to take it slow. But I guarantee I will never promise more than I can deliver and if I'm in service to you, you are the only person who will matter to me."

Sam chewed her pizza and studied her dinner companion. "After we're done eating, I want very much to take you home, tie you up, and abuse and ravish you. Would that be moving too quickly for you?"

Yen dropped her chin and blushed, red tinting her cheeks all the way to the tips of her ears. "No, Sir. Thank you, Sir," she whispered.

"I need to know your limits, hard and soft."

Yen shrugged. "I'm not really a masochist, more of a service submissive. With a long slow warm up, I can take a lot. Hard limits are just the usual: no drugs, scat, animals, children, or men."

"Tested?"

"Not recently. But I've not had sex since I lost my job and I got tested before I lost my insurance coverage." She looked up at Sam. "And, you Sir?"

"Get tested every six months unless I'm hitched. Always clean. Don't do drugs. And, my primary fetish is dacryphilia. So I don't need to hurt you as much as I need to make you cry."

"That shouldn't be difficult." Yen batted her eye lashes. "I can take a lot, but I'm a wuss."

"Can I get you ladies more beer?" Nicoli picked up their empty glasses.

"Just a box and the check." Sam grabbed the last bite of pizza from her plate.

Nicoli brought back a cardboard box and slid the remaining half of the pizza into it while Sam pulled four tens and a five out of her wallet, tossed them on the table, then grabbed the box with one hand and Yen's arm with the other.

When they emerged into the cooling summer night, Yen stuck her hand into Sam's pocket and hit the button on the truck remote. She opened Sam's door and held the pizza while she climbed inside. Sam waited until Yen had settled into the passenger side and buckled on her seatbelt before handing her the pizza box.

"Do you need to let your parents know you're not coming home tonight?" Sam headed the truck for the freeway.

Yen dropped her chin and whispered. "No, Sir. I called and told them I was spending the night with a girlfriend." She swallowed. "They don't know. They're still trying to fix me up with a nice boy and hoping for grandchildren."

"I'm not big on rug rats."

Yen laughed. "That's okay, neither am I. Although I do like working with teens and I volunteer at the queer center."

"Surprised we've never run into each other. I'm on the board." Sam put the truck in gear and headed for the street.

"I tend to avoid any events that might involve cameras. And, mostly I work with girls who haven't yet or are just coming out and aren't comfortable at the Center, so I meet them off site."

Sam gunned the truck up the freeway ramp and merged into traffic. The only hesitation she had about Yen was the girl seemed too good to be true. "How well do you know Julie?"

"Julie?"

"The bride of the bridal party that took over the spa to-day."

"The blonde with the bubble gum pink nail polish?"

Sam nodded and shifted to the fast lane. Out of the corner of her eye, she saw Yen shrug her shoulders.

"Done her once or twice. Seems nice enough, if a bit of a prima donna. Tips well. Why?"

Sam laughed. "Because she set us up."

"How? ... Why? ... What?" Yen sputtered.

Sam rested her right hand on Julie's slender thigh. "Don't panic. I was Julie's introduction to the concept of homosexuality and I knew I liked girls when I was four. She's developed the most highly-tuned gaydar of anyone I've ever known." Sam sniggered. "Of course, it was partially in self defense. Once Julie discovered, several years later, that she liked boys and that preferring girls was considered an aberration, she made a point of surrounding herself with straight girls. She's never given me shit about my orientation, but I swear she's half afraid if she has too many Lezzie friends she'll become Gay by association."

Yen giggled. "I've known women like that, but I refuse to be the token Lesbian friend."

"Normally, I feel the same way. But, Julie and I go way back -- we've known each other since we were two -- and she's the first person whose opinion of me didn't change once she found out I was different."

"Well, if she did deliberately fix us up, and I don't skew her ratio too badly, I guess I can make an exception."

"Good, because you might just have to be my date for her wedding."

Yen shuddered. "I despise weddings."

"Yeah, me too. But it was worth it to go along with the charade for the shock factor." Sam crossed back to the slow lane and headed down the exit ramp. At the light, she saw Yen had cocked her head to one side in question, her hair falling over the breasts Sam wanted so badly to plunder. "I'm wearing the same style tux as the best man and I insisted I only be referred to as the best woman."

Slowly, a smile spread Yen's lips across her face. "Sir, I imagine you will be quite handsome in a tuxedo. I would be delighted to accompany you, if you would like me to."

Sam maneuvered the truck down the side streets to her house and pulled into the driveway, waiting for Yen to jump out and open her door. Sliding out, she pulled Yen into her arms and pressed her length against the woman's softness. "You'll wear a pretty dress for me? Something feminine, but not too frilly?"

"I believe I have the perfect outfit."

Sam kissed her neck, reached back into the truck for the pizza, and pushed the door closed. With one arm around Yen's shoulders, she led her up the stairs on to the porch, releasing her only to unlock the door.

Inside, Sam flipped on the entry light. Yen dropped to her knees on the Persian carpet and planted a kiss on each of Sam's boots. Sam stuck out one foot and let Yen pull off her boot and sock. Before Sam could point, Yen found the leather slippers under the narrow wooden bench and kissed Sam's foot, her lips lingering against the skin, before putting the slipper on. By the time Yen had completed the ritual with her other foot, dampness had penetrated Sam's underwear.

Grabbing Yen's hair, she pulled her up and assaulted her lips with her own, biting the lower one until Yen cried out. She pulled the girl to her feet and dragged her to the door leading to the basement. Releasing her, Sam unlocked it and led Yen down the carpeted stairs. When she flipped the light switch at the bottom, Yen gasped.

Eyes wide, the girl turned around staring at the cross, spanking bench, bondage rack, massage table, and wall of whips, cuffs, paddles, and more. Yen edged toward the Queen-sized bed in the far corner. "Could we go straight to ravishing and skip the abuse?"

Sam laughed. "Don't worry, little one. I don't plan to use all of these on you at once." She frowned. "But, I don't allow girls in here unless they're naked."

Yen bowed and slowly unbuttoned her blouse, revealing a hint of red, but keeping it closed until it was undone. Then she eased the fabric apart a little at a time, uncovering mounds of creamy white skin restrained by blood red lace.

Sam flipped another switch, turning on the iPod speakers, suffusing the room with jazz guitar. Yen swayed with the rhythm, swinging her hips while she slid the blouse off and unfastened her pants. Removing her outer garments, she twirled around Sam wearing only her bra and the matching lace thong, the white globes of her ass taunting Sam until she reached out and grabbed them, pulling Yen against her.

With Sam clutching her cheeks, Yen reached behind her back and unlatched her bra, letting the cups drop away so her breasts landed against Sam's shirt. Holding onto Yen's ass, Sam lowered her mouth and licked her way down to Yen's succulent nipple. Pulling it into her mouth, Sam dug her nails into Yen's ass and pressed her teeth into her tit.

Yen cried out, but Sam could smell Yen's musk, mingled with the scent of her own. A tear slid off Yen's cheek and splashed onto her tit, and Sam's clit throbbed. She licked the salty sweetness back to its source, delighted to find more trickling from Yen's eyes.

Releasing one cheek while keeping her nails planted in the other, Sam grabbed Yen's tits, pinching the nipple between her thumb and forefinger until Yen's tears poured out. Sam growled and licked them off Yen's face, relishing the taste.

Without releasing her, Sam walked her back to the bed and fell onto it with her. She shoved Yen's nipple in her mouth and used that hand to reach for one of the cuff's attached with chains to the bed's feet.

"Please, Sir." Yen was panting. "May I have the honor of undressing you before you tie me up?"

Sam chuckled and bit into Yen's nipple before releasing it.

She sat up and let Yen unbutton her shirt. After pushing it back off Sam's arms, Yen lifted her white tee shirt over her head and licked her way from Sam's jaw line to her breasts, covering them with sloppy kisses.

Sam unbuttoned her jeans and Yen took the hint, kissing her way down and pulling Sam's pants off at the same time. Sam wriggled her hips to help and sighed when Yen kissed her way back up the inside of Sam's thighs. Yen paused with her nose above Sam's bush and inhaled. "Oh yum, Please, Sir may I?"

Sam pushed her hips up in response and Yen dove in. The girl had a talented and intuitive tongue. She licked and sucked Sam's clit and pushed her tongue into Sam's slit. She accurately read Sam's response, bringing her close to climax faster than any girl Sam had ever been with.

Pushing Yen's head tighter into her crotch, pressing her hips up into the woman's wonderful mouth, Sam let herself fall into the building tension. Yen sucked Sam's clit into her mouth, pushing at it with her tongue, and eased her fingers into Sam's sopping wet cunt, pushing up against her G-spot until Sam convulsed and growled in satisfaction.

Yen kissed her way up to Sam's neck and nestled against her shoulder, licking the dripping juices off her lips. Sam rolled her over on her back and clipped the cuffs first to her wrists and then to her ankles.

Splayed across the bed, her face still slick with Sam's come, her heavy breathing jiggling her magnificent breasts, Yen stared at Sam, eyes wide. Sam pushed herself off the bed and yanked open a drawer in the tall wooden chest against the wall. She extracted her largest FeelDoe, slammed the drawer shut, and grabbed a deer hide flogger from the wall.

Returning to the bed, she swung the whip, caressing Yen's mounds, flat stomach, and slender thighs with the tails.

Yen's breathing sped up. Sam increased the strength behind her throws, the slap of the leather matching the pace of Yen's respiration. When Sam put real force behind the flogger, slapping Yen's luscious tits, the girl's lower lip trembled and tears spilled from her eyes. Dropping the flogger on the bed, Sam jammed the short end of the FeelDoe into her still-dripping cunt, and plunged the longer end into Yen. The woman moaned, and pushed her hips up to meet Sam's onslaught.

Sam drove herself into the girl again and again until her second orgasm reverberated through her. "You may come, girl" she growled and Yen trembled beneath her, sobbing. Her tears just added to the exquisite tension in Sam's clit and she increased the force of her thrusts until she collapsed in a third orgasm.

When her breath slowed to just faster than normal, she reached over Yen's head and unclipped the cuffs. Easing down beside her, Sam gathered her into her arms. Yen nuzzled her nose against Sam's neck and purred. "Thank you so much, Sir. I hope you were pleased with me."

Sam chuckled. "So, tell me, my pretty, about this perfect outfit you're thinking of wearing to Julie's wedding?"

Salt for His Wounds

By I.G. Frederick

I opened the front door and had to hang onto it for support. My ex-husband stood on the porch with a little-boy-lost look on his face that did nothing to enhance his forty-five-year-old features. Geez, he even had flowers in his hands -- red roses, my favorites. Too bad he had never brought me any when we were still married.

"What do you want?" I peered into the soulful brown eyes that used to send shivers down my spine, relieved that I still felt nothing.

He held out the flowers. "Could I come in?" He looked a bit leaner than when we parted for the last time, almost a year ago. His beard showed a little more grey, but the hair fringing his naked scalp was still almost all black.

"No." I ignored the roses.

"Please, Eleanor." His voice whined and grated. "I made a mistake. I'm sorry. Can't we talk?"

"I have nothing I want to talk about with you." My voice was as cold as my heart. I wasn't angry, I didn't hate him; I just didn't care anything about him anymore. I don't know when I stopped loving him. At some point, after fifteen years, I realized I just didn't anymore.

I broke the news to him one rainy Sunday afternoon in January. He didn't take it well. I suggested we get counseling, to try and figure out what went wrong. He didn't entertain that suggestion for even a minute. "If you don't love me, what's the point?" Now here he stood on my porch in the afternoon sun wanting "to talk."

"Look, I know we should have had this conversation a year ago." His voice had lost the grating edge, but it still jolted me out of my memories. "But I was just so hurt when you told me you didn't love me anymore." Well, I suppose he was. But maybe I hurt, too. Maybe I was tired of being taken for granted and endless sexual frustration. "You were the woman I planned to spend the rest of my life with. I reacted badly. Please, Eleanor, give me another chance."

I sighed. "I've moved on with my life, Donald. It's time for you to do the same." I had, too, in a big way. I had packed up everything and left Portland where I'd spent most of my life. Now I lived a hundred and fifty miles away in a tiny little town on the central Oregon coast. I had found a cozy townhouse overlooking the ocean and bought it for cash with my half of the marital assets. I was quite content doing freelance graphic design work from home, making just enough to pay the bills. I didn't miss our high-stress, big-house-in-the-west-hills lifestyle.

"I can't, Eleanor, not without you." A tear crept down his cheek.

"Well, you're going to have to find a way to build a new life for yourself. We're divorced now, remember. I told you if we ended the relationship it would be permanent and complete. I have no room in my life for you now." Living by myself, although lonely, was a definite improvement over what living with Donald had become. I had no interest in going back.

"Look, I understand you don't love me anymore. But surely you miss Portland -- the theater, the restaurants, the excitement? You could move back in with me. We could have our old life back."

Maybe, if he'd suggested this a year ago ... but now I wouldn't consider his offer for even a second. "No, Donald, I don't miss Portland. And, I don't miss you."

He winced. "Have you found someone else?" The pain in his eyes almost made me feel sorry for him. Almost.

"That's none of your business." I hadn't -- you don't meet too many men if the only time you leave the house is to walk on the beach alone or go to the grocery store -- but I wasn't about to let him know that. I thought he would cry and I didn't want to see it. "Go back to Portland, Donald." I closed the door and returned to work.

Engrossed in coding HTML, I forgot about Donald. But about an hour later, when I emerged from my spare-bedroom/office to get a soda, I looked out the window to see he still sat in the corner of the porch, the roses across his knees. *Shit*, I thought. *He's going to start stalking me now.*

I carried my soda back to the office and pondered the situation for a few minutes. Donald had always been stubborn. He truly had been a forever kind of guy. The only way to get him off my porch was to convince him that I had found another man. I picked up the phone and dialed my next-door neighbor's number.

"Mick," I said when he answered. "I need a REALLY big favor." Mick worked out of his home also -- for a high-tech firm in the San Francisco Bay area. His company, and his job, had survived all the cutbacks and the recession. He was probably fifteen years younger than I. We met the day I moved in, although I had seen him before, when I first looked at the place. He had helped me unpack and install my computer and some other electronics. Since then we had become pretty good friends. He fed my cats when I visited my folks in Portland; I took care of his dog when he traveled on business. We often shared meals and even occasionally went up to Newport for an evening out.

Although we seemed to have a lot in common, I knew we would never share more than friendship. The guy was drop-dead gorgeous: green eyes that reminded me of emeralds, thick dark blond hair that swept his shoulders, and a physique that would make any woman wet with desire. His arms and chest rippled with muscles and he had the legs of an athlete. At one time, I had seriously considered drilling a hole through our adjoining walls so I could see what he had inside his shorts. In all our conversations about every topic under the sun, the one I avoided scrupulously was relationships. I didn't want to know anything about his love life.

"What's up?" he asked. His light tone indicated that the interruption was not an imposition. We had, I realized, become a little dependent on each other. I relied on Mick to fix my computer when it went haywire and he occasionally needed me to help him with the numerous PowerPoint slides he had to generate for work. But was this too much to ask?

"See that guy sitting on my porch?" I waited while Mick wandered into his kitchen with his portable phone.

"A suitor?" His tone teased. Mick knew I was divorced, but that was all he knew.

"No, my ex."

"Is he bothering you?" He sounded concerned. "Do you want me to scare him off?" That wouldn't be hard for Mick; he was at least half a foot taller than Donald and much more muscular. Donald was pudgy and not terribly strong. But I knew that physical intimidation would not have the effect of the scheme I had concocted.

"Well, yes and no." I hesitated. I must have lost my senses, asking Mick to do this. He would think I was coming on to him and laugh in my face. I'm not ugly, but I'm not a young beauty anymore either. My auburn hair has several grey streaks and I probably could stand to lose another ten pounds. Giving up my sixty-hour-a-week, high-stress, web design job had allowed me the time to start working out again. I had lost twenty pounds and toned up quite a bit since I left Portland. Mick had converted his one-car garage into a mini-gym -- no health club in our little town -- and let me use it as much as I wanted. Not eating lunch and dinner at restaurants almost every day helped too. Still, I always felt dowdy next to Mick.

"I was wondering if you would be willing to come over here and pretend you're my lover." I rushed the words out before I could change my mind. "I think that's the only thing that's going to convince him to leave and not come back."

The other end of the phone was silent for a long time. At least he wasn't laughing. Probably thinking of a polite way to turn me down.

"Look, forget it," I said, ashamed I had even asked. I could feel the heat on my cheeks and knew my face was beet red. "It was a stupid idea anyway. If I ignore him, he'll go away eventually."

"No, I think you're right." Mick's voice had a funny hitch in it. He probably agreed to go along with me against his better judgment, a true friend. "It's probably the best way to make him realize he has no future with you. I assume that's the message you want to deliver?"

"Yes."

"I'll be there in a few minutes." The phone went dead with a click.

Oh, geez, I thought, what have I done now? I ducked into the bathroom, looked in the mirror, and regretted my impulsive invitation. I wore my standard work clothes of sweats and an old t-shirt. I wanted to change into something sexy, but realized if I did, Donald would likely notice and he might figure out my scheme. Besides, Mick knew what I wore to work. We had lunch together often enough. I didn't want him to think I looked for more than a ruse to get rid of my ex-husband.

When I heard his knock, I went back to the kitchen. Mick stood at the door, gorgeous as ever. Donald, at the far end of the porch, glared at him.

"I decided to take the rest of the afternoon off," he said, as if we hadn't spoken on the phone a minute ago. Mick leaned down, kissed me, and wrapped his arms around my waist. Then he stood up straight so my feet dangled, and walked into the house with me pressed against his chest. He pushed the door closed with his back. My arms had found their way around his neck and my fingers ran through his glorious silky hair. I realized I was breathing heavily and Mick's tongue was in my mouth. I could taste the coffee that he consumed by the gallon.

Mick set me on the kitchen counter but didn't release me. Standing between my legs, he held me tight with one arm while the other hand found its way to my head. He wove his fingers through my hair as he pressed my mouth harder against his. *This boy knew how to pretend.* My eyes were closed, but I looked out through my lashes and saw Donald pressed against the window, a hand on either side of his eyes so he could see inside. *Let's give the man a show.*

I let my hands drift down, enjoying the feel of Mick's muscular back. From this position I could barely reach his ass, but I stretched to grab his cheeks and squeezed. He pressed himself against me and I was surprised to feel he was hard under his denim shorts. *Maybe poor Mick hadn't gotten any for a while.* I wondered if pretending turned him on enough, whether he would settle for me in a pinch.

Mick's mouth had left my lips and drifted down my neck. I let my head fall back, reveling in the silky touch of his tongue. "Wrap your legs around me," he whispered, his breath hot on my sensitive skin. I did, sliding my arms up out of the way and back around his neck. He started toward the bedroom with me attached to his chest. *Oh well, show's over.*

When we reached my bedroom, I reluctantly let my legs slip down Mick's backside and prepared for him to release me. But his lips still traveled up and down my neck and his hand reached under my t-shirt for my breast.

"You can stop pretending now," my voice was hoarse. "Donald can't see us in here."

"Who's pretending?" His voice had that funny hitch in it again.

Mick lifted my shirt over my breasts and buried his face in my rather ample cleavage. His fingers fumbled behind my back with the clasp of my bra. I was panting.

"I don't have any protection." I knew I didn't want him to stop, but I also was afraid his regret afterwards would end our friendship. As much as I wanted Mick to make love to me, I didn't want to lose him as a friend. The lack of birth control would give him an easy out.

With my bra undone, Mick pushed the fabric up so he could reach my nipple with his mouth. He still had one arm around my waist, holding me tight against him, while he fumbled in the pocket of his shorts with the other. His hand came out with a strip of six condoms. If he hadn't been holding me I would have fallen to the floor. This was not a case of physical contact getting out of hand. Men might carry a rubber in their wallets, but they don't run around with a pocket full.

Sensing my knees had given out, Mick picked me up and gently laid me on my bed, pulling my bra and t-shirt over my head. He kicked off his shoes and stretched out beside me, a hand on one breast and his mouth firmly attached to the other. As his tongue rolled my hardening nipple around in his mouth, his other hand played with my hair, his thumb caressing my face and lips. I moaned. At least two years had passed since a man had made love to me -- Donald gave up sex long before we decided to separate. My skin burned everywhere Mick touched me.

I tried to unbutton his shirt, I wanted to feel Mick's skin against mine, but I couldn't get my fingers to work. Mick chuckled and got off the bed. My body cried out in agony for his touch. One by one, he undid the buttons of his shirt and let it fall to the floor. Then he reached for his shorts. He had a wicked glint in his eye as if he knew I enjoyed the show. He unbuttoned the waistband and lowered the zipper so slowly I wanted to scream. Finally he opened it and pushed his shorts and briefs down his hips and legs. His dick jumped out and I reached out my hand, wanting so much just to touch it. As beautiful as the rest of him, it was long and thick with a won-derfully smooth head.

Pushing my hand away, Mick knelt beside the bed and put his mouth back on my breast. Then his lips slid down across my chest and stomach as his hands pulled my sweats and panties out of his mouth's way. I lifted my hips so he could get them off and gasped when his tongue found its way between my legs. He pulled one leg over his shoulder and pushing into my cunt with his tongue, teasing my clito-ris, driving me mad. I had three orgasms before he kissed his way back up to my breasts.

He slipped his sheathed cock inside me. Somehow, he had managed to get a rubber on while I was too busy coming to notice. I moaned. He was big and being full felt so good. Mick was probably twice as thick and half again as long as Donald -- who always expected me to put it in for him -- and I could feel the head pushing against my cervix. When Mick was all the way inside me, he stayed there for a minute, letting me get used to the glorious feeling. I wrapped my legs around his waist. Then he pulled back until only the head was inside and thrust it in again, his balls slapping my ass and his pelvis grinding into my clit. I could feel another climax starting to build as Mick slammed into me over and over. This time I screamed. If Donald still waited out on the porch, I'm sure he got an earful to go with the eyeful he had gotten earlier.

I came hard, and my head bounced up and down on the pillow. Mick kept pumping into me and my orgasm wouldn't stop. I just kept coming until I couldn't hold on anymore and my legs and arms slipped back down onto the bed. At that moment, Mick's eyes closed and his lips clamped down on mine as he shot his load. Even with my pussy still pulsing I could feel his cock throbbing inside me. I sucked greedily on his tongue until he collapsed onto me. He still had most of his weight on his forearms, but his chest pressed against mine. He kissed my eyes, my nose, my cheeks, my lips. I looked into those beautiful green eyes and I was amazed at the passion I saw.

Mick stayed on top of me, kissing me, until he started to slip out. Then he grabbed his rubber, pulled it off, tied a knot in the end, and tossed it into the wastebasket on the other side of the room. He lay back down beside me and cradled me in his arms. I waited for him to fall asleep, or get up and get dressed to leave, but he didn't. He just held me, my head on his shoulder, his arms pulling me tight against his side. I didn't want to break the spell, but I had to know.

"What just happened here?"

"That's not a very nice question to ask a man who just made love to you for an hour." Mick smiled. I looked at the clock. I hadn't realized that much time had passed.

"I wasn't referring to your lovemaking. That was wonderful." I lifted my head and kissed him on his lips. I had only intended to give him a grateful smack, but before I knew it I had stretched out across his chest, his arms holding me against him, and our tongues dancing in each other's mouths. Better yet, I could feel him getting hard again between my legs. Donald's idea of a sex life, before he lost interest entirely, was twice a month. I don't think we ever did it more than once in the same day, even when we were first married.

I decided Mick deserved a taste of his own medicine, so I reluctantly pulled my lips from his and let my mouth explore his wonderful, muscular body. I lingered a bit to tease his hardened nipples and was rewarded with a soft, pleasurable sigh. His chest was practically hairless, just a little patch of blond bristles between his nipples and a trace leading down to his pubic hair. By the time I got there, he pointed straight up and I covered his pole and balls with kisses. The sigh was louder this time.

I licked the full length of the shaft, up and down until I had worked my way in a complete circle, careful to over-lap so I wouldn't miss an inch of him, slurping in his sticky sweetness. Then I took the head in my mouth and slowly eased my lips as far down his length as I could go. This time he moaned. Raking my teeth gently along his shaft as I rose up, I paused to nibble the head. Then I started working my mouth up and down his length, tonguing the head on the up stroke. His hips moved with my rhythm and his fingers played with my hair.

He tried to pull my ass up to his face, but I resisted. I've never liked sixty-nine. When I have a face in my pussy I want to lay back and enjoy it. When I've got a dick in my mouth I want to concentrate on pleasing it. With Donald, this was never an issue. I don't think he went down on me more than a dozen times in the fifteen years we were married. I stopped giving him head when I realized he had no intention of re-ciprocating and I had forgotten just how good a mouthful of cock tasted.

The muscles in Mick's legs and ass tightened and he tugged on my hair, trying to get me to stop. "I don't want to come without you," he said through gritted teeth. I spotted the rest of the condoms on the floor and grabbed the strip. Pulling one wrapper open I took out the sheath and rolled it down over Mick's massive cock. Then I positioned my hips over his and lowered myself onto him. We both moaned as the exquisite sensation overwhelmed us. Mick reached up and fondled my breasts. I leaned forward on my arms and began sliding up and down his long pole, rubbing my clit against him in between strokes.

I watched Mick's face. His eyes were partially open, but I could only see the whites. His lips parted and his nostrils flared. He raised and lowered his hips, thrusting up into my down stroke. I could feel my orgasm building, but I didn't want to come yet. The delicious sensation of mounting tension, combined with the glorious hardness of his cock filling my wet pussy, felt too good. I stopped moving for a moment and sat up. I clenched and unclenched my pussy muscles around Mick's cock. A big grin spread across his face and he looked up at me with eyes glazed over by lust.

Releasing my breasts, he sat up and wrapped his arms around me. He started rocking back and forth. Now I rolled my eyes back inside my head. My clit was getting over stimulated and I lost all control. I think this orgasm lasted longer than the one before. When I started coming, Mick slid his legs over the edge of the bed and lifted me up and down on his cock. I was still coming when he exploded inside me. The two of us held onto each other until my throbbing stopped. I couldn't move. Mick laid me back across the bed, got rid of the condom and then took me in his arms again. I would have been perfectly happy to just stay like this forever.

"To answer your question...," Mick paused.

Talk about a delayed reaction.

"I've wanted you from the first day you moved in here. At the time, I thought you might still be getting over your divorce. You didn't talk about it much and I figured maybe you were still kind of raw, so I gave you some time." I managed to get my head off his shoulder long enough to look him in the eye. He was serious. This hunk of a man was attracted to me. How had I missed that?

"Then we started to become friends and, well, you never seemed interested in going any further than that. I was afraid if I made a pass at you and you turned me down you'd be reluctant to continue our friendship." Mick stroked my hair with one hand while the other played with my tit. "You don't know how many times I jacked off pretending I was playing with these." He squeezed my breast.

"Anyway, when you called today, at first I was afraid I couldn't help you. I didn't think I could pretend to be your lover without getting carried away." He leaned over and planted a quick kiss on my nipple. "Then I realized you'd just handed me the perfect opportunity. Worst case scenario, if you weren't interested you'd let me know and I would apologize for getting into my role too much and we'd be able to continue where we left off. But if by any chance you might be attracted to me, this was my one hope of finding out." He shifted slightly and gently pressed his lips to mine for a moment. "I should send your ex-husband a thank you card."

"That would be rubbing salt in his wounds," I scolded. But, I had to admit, I was grateful Donald had showed up. To think, Mick and I been fantasizing about each other all this time. For all I knew, we could have been having mutual orgasms without even realizing it.

I lay in Mick's arms without speaking. I was drifting, almost asleep, when Mick cleared his throat. "Eleanor, I know you haven't seen anyone since you moved here." I looked at him in alarm. Had he been spying on me? "You almost never leave your house except when you walk on the beach and the only visitors I've seen until today were your folks."

I guess we live close enough to know each other's business. I was well aware that he never had women over, but I just figured he went to their places -- and I didn't really want to know anyway. He was right about my social life, though. I had turned into a hermit. He probably was the only person in town with whom I had exchanged more than four words at a time. I settled back onto his shoulder.

"Was this just because you haven't had sex in so long?" He swallowed. "I mean, you never expressed any interest in me before."

I lifted my head once more and looked at him in amazement. I wanted to cry. He looked so vulnerable, as if he had bared his soul to me and was afraid I would slash it open.

"One of the reasons I bought this place is because I liked the scenery," I ran my hand up and down the muscular expanse of his chest, "and I'm not referring to the ocean view." Mick had been working on his truck, naked from the waist up, the day the realtor showed me my townhouse for the first time. Whenever I looked at other places, I couldn't get that picture out of my mind.

"I've had the hots for you from the first moment I saw you, but I always figured I was too old for you. I kept my feelings to myself because I didn't need another rejection." Nothing like having her own husband turn her down to smash a woman's self esteem.

His eyes lit up with delight and all traces of vulnerability disappeared. "You've got to be kidding. Just how young do you think I am?"

"I figure you can't be more than twenty five." My hand still roamed across the muscles of his chest. His breathing was even, but his nipples had hardened again.

"I'm thirty-one, silly." Okay, so he was only nine years younger than me, not fifteen. "The same age as you."

My hand stopped and I looked into his amazing eyes. "Wherever did you get the idea that I was thirty-one?" I suppose I should be flattered, but now I could only worry how he would react to the difference in our ages.

"Aren't you? I mean your hair's a little grey, but being married to an old fuddy-duddy like Donald could do that to you." Mick shifted his weight so he was on his side looking down at me. "You don't have any wrinkles." He traced my eyes and my lips with his fingers. "And you're in great shape. I don't like women who are so skinny their bones press into you when you make love to them." His hand slid down my neck, along my breasts, and across my belly. "Women are supposed to be soft."

I may as well get this over with. It was nice while it lasted. "I'm thirty-nine years old, Mick, I'll be forty in three months."

His expression didn't change; his hand kept wandering, exploring my body with long, soft fingers. "Nope, not a day over thirty-one," he said as if he hadn't heard my confession.

I started to protest, but he covered my mouth with his -- a soft, gentle kiss with only a hint of the passion we had shared such a short while ago. His lips worked their way down my jaw to my neck.

"Aren't we a pair of fools?" His hot breath caressed my skin. A few moments passed before it sank in -- he didn't care one little bit how old I was. His mouth found its way back to my breast and we both started breathing heavily. I tangled my fingers in his silky hair and pulled his face toward mine.

"I guess we'll just have to work harder to make up for lost time," I whispered before our mouths clamped together again.

Proposal
What a Tangled Web We Weave

By I.G. Frederick

Through the glass, Geraldine watched the tall dark-skinned man stride across the parking garage toward the restaurant elevator. Dressed up for the occasion, he wore a black jacket, black shirt, and white tie. At better than six-feet tall, Christopher's height almost overwhelmed her when they were together, even though she was almost five seven herself. But he was the sweetest, gentlest man she had ever met and she had come to love him dearly over the last six months.

Three of her friends were betting that Christopher would propose tonight. He'd made reservations at one of the most elegant restaurants in town and told her they needed to have a serious discussion. But Geraldine suspected something else. Despite his charm, she sensed Chris was keeping something secret from her. She hoped tonight he would tell her what so she could decide whether or not it was a deal breaker.

"Wow, you look fantastic, Gerry." Chris leaned down to kiss her on the cheek.

She turned her face so their lips met, bracing herself with a hand on his muscular arm for the thrill his touch sent through her body. Mint mouthwash on his breath tickled her nose, adding to the sensory deluge. The past three days she'd tried to imagine what he could be hiding from her, hoping it wouldn't destroy their relationship. She had never enjoyed a man's company as much as Christopher's, but if his secret was so devastating he believed he couldn't confide in her ... well, she would suffer less if she broke it off now.

Roger was convinced Chris was still married Loretta certain he'd decided he was gay, despite Gerry's reports of amazing sexual chemistry. And, of course everyone else believed he had planned some sort of elaborate, romantic proposal.

Chris offered her his arm and they rode up thirty floors. The elevator doors slid open and a wave of tantalizing aromas washed over them -- garlic and ginger, sizzling steak, and fried seafood. The waiter led them to a table covered in crisp white linen next to the wall of windows. With the city straddling the river far below them, Gerry silently wished the majority of her friends were correct, even though until she met Chris she had no interest in getting married again.

Chris let the view hold his attention, sharing his observations about various landmarks, until their drinks arrived. He toyed with his martini glass, twirling the yellow concoction around and around while she sipped at the combination of fruit juices and rum in her mai tai.

"Geraldine, I don't know if you realize how fond I've become of you."

Interesting choice of words, fond. And using her full name didn't bode well.

"I really would like to take our relationship to the next level." He gulped down half his margarita in one swallow.

"But?" She plucked the cherry from her glass and bit it off the stem.

He rested his folded hands on the table. "But, I've been married twice before, and I've finally learned that without certain," he cleared his throat, "elements, I can't..." he took another gulp, "I just can't."

Does that mean you want to marry me, if...? "Perhaps you should tell me what these "elements" are?" She drew air quotes.

"Can I interest you two in some appetizers? Some Black Tiger Shrimp Tempura or a Spicy Yellowfin Tuna Roll?"

What timing. "Could you give us a few minutes?"She tapped the thick leather volume in front of her. "We haven't even had a chance to look at the menu."

The waiter disappeared and Gerry scrutinized Chris, tilting her head to one side.

He leaned forward and whispered, "I'm a pervert."

"That's rather a broad classification. Can you be more specific?"

His chin dropped to his chest. She could see his mouth move, but couldn't hear his words over the tinkle of piano music from the bar and the chatter of other diners.

"Would you like to text it to me?"

She *was* joking, but gratitude infused his features and he grinned, pulling out his cell. Gerry had turned off her ringer, but she extracted her phone from her purse and stared wide-eyed at the message he sent.

"I take it from your expression, this is not something you've been involved in before?" His deep voice broke through her shock.

She shook her head and took a long swallow of rum-infused fruit juice. Opening her menu, she blinked until she could focus on the words. "Maybe we should order some food?" She didn't think alcohol caused her dizziness, but putting something substantial in her stomach wouldn't hurt.

They stared out the window without speaking until the waiter set a plate of Kung Pao Calamari on the table between them and the scent of onions and ginger steamed around her. Gerry speared a ring and dipped it into the Hoisin sauce before popping it into her mouth. The spicy combination woke up her senses and her curiosity. "How much do you need this? Just in the bedroom or all the time?"

Chris blinked rapidly, staring at her. "I could settle for the former, but would much prefer the latter."

She took another succulent piece of the breaded calamari and skipped the spicy sauce. Chris sat with his hands in his lap, avoiding her eyes.

"You should try these, they're delicious."

"Thank you." He pulled a few pieces onto his plate and spooned some of the sauce over them. He swallowed and looked at her with pleading eyes. "Would you consider ...?" He pressed his thick lips together.

She took a deep breath. "I don't know much about it."

He grinned, revealing white, even teeth. "I could teach you. There are all kinds of books, I have more than a few myself. And there's groups in town where you could meet others who ..."

She cleared her throat. "*If* I decide to explore this, I prefer we keep it between us." She couldn't even imagine telling her friends, never mind joining a group with a bunch of strangers.

"If that's what you wish, Ma'am."

Gerry blinked rapidly, trying to find her equilibrium and seriously considered a trip to the ladies' room that ended at the elevator. "Let's stick to names, for now. At least in public."

Disappointment flashed across his face, but he swallowed and it disappeared.

When their entrées arrived, Chris sat with his hands on his lap while Gerry cut into her macadamia encrusted pork chop and savored flavors of rich nuts and tender meat drizzled with vanilla infused passion fruit sauce. She helped herself to a taste of Chris's goat cheese and prosciutto stuffed chicken and sampled his buttermilk mashed potatoes with lemon garlic jus that melted on her tongue. "Not bad. You'll like it."

Only then, did he pick up his knife and fork. She took a deep breath at the implications. *You can do this.*

When the waiter brought the dessert menus, Chris left his sitting on the table. Gerry tilted her head, but he stared at his hands. She couldn't decide between the coconut marjolaine and the crème brûlée so she ordered one for herself and one for Chris. After tasting both, twice, she traded the plates so he had the crème brûlée. He raised his eyes, she nodded, and he dipped his spoon into the creamy concoction.

Gerry was surprised to realize her breathing had become shallow and her heart was racing. More than anything else, she wanted to take Chris home and rip off his clothes. After he paid the bill, she rose to her feet and strode toward the elevator. She heard his heavy footsteps following her and they rode down to the garage in silence.

He handed her into his red Acura and slid behind the wheel. "Where to, Ma'am?"

She took a deep breath. "If we go back to your place, will I be surprised by things you haven't shown me before besides these books you apparently have stashed away somewhere?"

He looked down. "Yes, Ma'am."

"Don't think I'm ready for that. Take me home."

His lips tightened in a grimace, but he started the car, backed out, and headed toward the exit.

Watching the line of red lights stretch out in front of them across the Burnside Bridge and the white lights coming in the other direction, Gerry wondered if she was cut out for the kind of relationship Chris said he wanted. For that matter, he seemed too willful, independent, and stubborn. One thing to have a man willingly "devote myself to your pleasure," as he'd texted. Another to force him to obey.

When he pulled up in front of her building's entrance, Chris spoke for the first time since he'd started the car. "Would, Ma'am like me to come in after I park?"

"You'd better." Whatever the evening's outcome, Gerry intended to at least get laid.

By the time she unlocked her condo, turned on the lights, and closed all the window blinds, Chris stood in the doorway. She tilted her head to look up at him. "Aren't you supposed to be on your knees or something?"

He closed the door. "Yes, Ma'am. Would you like me naked, as well."

Gerry smiled. "Why not?"

Chris loosened his tie, removed his jacket, and slipped out of the black silk shirt that clung to his lean torso. Hanging them all on one arm of her bentwood coat tree, he stripped down to black bikini briefs and socks, then lowered himself to his knees.

Gerry pointed at his crotch. "I think you forgot something."

Chris's wide nose flared. She found his fear incredibly endearing. He added his briefs to the pile on the tree and stuffed his socks in his shoes. His cock pointed straight out at her and Gerry licked her lips.

After he knee-walked over to her, Chris leaned over, and kissed her feet. The touch of his lips on the skin exposed by the slinky sandals she still wore, sent a charge coursing through Gerry. Suppressing a shudder, she grabbed his ear and pulled him up so she could look into his dark brown eyes.

She leaned down to kiss him and he tilted his head back. On a whim, she bit his lower lip, sinking her teeth into the thick moist flesh. She wasn't sure which surprised her more, his reaction or hers. He moaned and swayed, his eyes rolling back into his head. Her panties got wet and she shivered with need. Realizing if she wanted to have sex with Chris all she had to do was demand it, Gerry tightened her grip on his ear and dragged him toward the bedroom. Despite staying on his knees, Chris kept up with her. She wondered if he would get rug burns, then decided she didn't care. *He's the one who wants this.*

Gerry sat on the edge of the bed and raised her feet off the floor. Chris slipped off first one sandal and then the other, slowly kissing each foot from toes to ankle as he did so, caressing her skin with his lips. Now her eyes were the ones rolling back. Her breathing came in audible gasps. Chris looked up with a glint in his eye, one corner of his mouth raised higher than the other.

He dragged a finger from her ankle to the top of her thigh. "Would Ma'am like me to continue?"

She hooked one foot behind his head and pulled him closer. Starting at her knees, he licked every inch of her bare skin until, burying his head under the narrow skirt of her black dress, he finally reached her soaked panties and inhaled deeply. Even she could smell her arousal. She lifted her hips and he dragged the black cotton slowly down her legs. She draped her thighs over his shoulders, pressing her heels against his naked back, urging him forward.

One of the things she had always loved about sex with Chris was his appetite for oral, but he outdid himself tonight. He engulfed her clit in his thick lips until she cried out, then he pushed his tongue deep into her. In the past she felt guilty about how long his face stayed between her legs sending her into paroxysm of pleasure. She always believed she had to give as much as she took. But, now she just reveled in the attention, letting him lick her lips inside and out, nuzzle her clit with his tongue, and thrust its entire length into the heat of her core.

When her clit throbbed at the edge of over sensitivity, she pushed him away with her feet against on his shoulders. He sat back on his heels and licked her juices off his lips. "Thank you, Ma'am, that was delicious." His cock still pointed straight up.

Gerry just stared at him, wondering what he would do if she crawled under the covers and went to sleep.

"Would Ma'am like me to give her a massage? Or a bath? Perhaps, she wishes to go to sleep while keeping me available to serve her in the morning? I make a mean omelette."

As tempting as his suggestions sounded, there was only one thing Gerry wanted at the moment. She opened the drawer of the nightstand, dug out a condom, and tossed it at him.

"Yes, Ma'am. Thank you, Ma'am."

She sat up and eased her slinky black dress over her head, tossing it onto the arm chair in the corner. Still wearing her bra slip, she got up on her knees and patted the bed. Chris stretched out on his back and she threw one leg over his hips. He ran his hands up her thighs and caressed her ass through the silky fabric of her slip. With one hand, Gerry rubbed the head of his cock against her clit and trembled at her reaction. Already hypersensitive, the soft skin of his glans against her swollen flesh almost sent her over the edge again.

Unable to resist any longer, she guided him into position and sank down onto his cock, sighing with pleasure. For a moment, she stayed still, reveling in the sensations of a full pussy, his coarse pubic hair tickling her lips. She admired the lean muscular body between her legs with the new understanding that it was available to serve her every whim. A wide grin split his face and he looked up at her adoringly.

Already floating in post-orgasmic euphoria from the magic he worked with his tongue, she didn't have the strength to move. "Make me come."

"Yes, Ma'am. Thank you, Ma'am."

Holding onto her hips, Chris raised and lowered himself, pushing up into her. She smiled. This pervert stuff had some definite benefits. He maneuvered his big hand so he could tease her clit with his thumb while moving his hips up and down so he massaged her internally with his cock. Gerry groaned, finding it more and more difficult to stay upright. When he sent her trembling off into another orgasm, she collapsed on his chest. He stroked her ass and back until she stopped shaking.

Unable to open her eyes, Gerry slid off him onto the bed. Using Chris's shoulder as a pillow while his hand caressed her backside, she found herself drifting toward sleep. With difficulty, she managed to open one eye wide enough to see his sheathed erection still pointing straight up. A smile tickled her lips.

Tomorrow she would have to get a list of the "all kinds of books" Chris had mentioned so she could learn more about this pervert stuff. But, she was pretty sure she liked the concept and if she allowed Chris to marry her, she'd be the wife he stuck with.

Starting Over

By I.G. Frederick

I felt like a ten-year-old who had entered a chocolate shop and found every case had a "free" label on it. When I walked into the brightly lit dungeon, I discovered two dozen naked boys, in every size from skinny to huge, kneeling in a row on the thick carpet. They ranged in age from early twenties to late fifties. I stuffed my canvass duffle into one of the cubbyholes near the entrance so I could survey the goodies.

At that moment, I finally forgave my friend Paula for coercing me into attending this event. Since my own pet had walked out on me four months ago, I'd stayed home from all the parties and anything else lifestyle related. I found it difficult to spend time with friends who complained about their submissives' minor misdeeds when mine had committed the ultimate transgression. It hurt to watch other women playing with their toys when I didn't have one of my own.

Here, though, any FemDom could claim one of the proffered toys for the evening. I recognized some of the boys who were owned by women I knew, on loan for the event. A few had no owners, and many of them I had never seen before. Some of those looked rather cute.

The large room -- bigger than my entire apartment -- had St. Andrews' crosses, bondage tables, cages, spanking benches, a suspension rig, and a sling. Posters on the blood red walls showed both male and female submissives in various bondage positions. Techno music played in the background.

I wore a one-piece leather corset dress that I had found at a thrift store for only twenty dollars. That, with black stockings and three-inch heels, made me feel sexier than I had in a long time. Before I could give the boy toys more than a cursory glance, Paula, Angeline, and Barbara embraced me with enthusiasm.

Angeline adjusted the bottom of her leather corset. "We're so glad to see you back in circulation."

Barbara put a latex-encased arm across my shoulders. "That boy didn't deserve you."

Of course Paula gloated. "Bet you're glad you came." She waved an arm toward the lineup. "Surely there's someone there you want to take home."

"I'll be satisfied if I have a toy to play with for the evening." I had no idea where Paula got the idea that I could find someone I wanted to collar so easily. I had spent months online and interviewing prospects before I found Richard. "I haven't had anyone to abuse in so long."

Angeline couldn't resist getting her digs in. "Perhaps if you selected someone closer to your own age, you might have more luck, long term."

I extricated myself from my friends to avoid spitting at her and greeted other FemDoms I knew. Then, I turned my attention to the boys on display. Each wore a play collar from which dangled a three-by-five tag on which they, or their owners, had written a list of "activities" in which they were willing to participate.

They all kept their eyes down and their chins on their chests, so I couldn't really see any of their faces. After months without a toy to play with, I found their equipment of more interest, anyway. I skipped over the pudgy boys, the older ones, and anyone who wasn't at least partially erect. Cock and ball torture is probably my favorite sadistic activity, but it really isn't any fun with a limp prick. And the bigger the toy, the more skin to hurt.

A well-endowed, tanned, blond youth -- he looked about twenty-three -- caught my eye. He had written CBT at the top of his tag in bold black letters and put the blindfold sticker at the bottom of his list. His engorged cock pointed at my feet. With a wicked grin on my face, I stepped behind the line. The blond had a gorgeous ass as well.

I knew this was one of the few opportunities I would have to play with such a luscious toy. At his age, with his looks, he could find a younger, prettier Domme, anytime he wanted. I'm pushing forty and have to use dye to keep the grey out of my red hair. While I don't exactly qualify as a BBW, I'm no size ten either. I figured, I might as well claim someone who would look good at my feet and had the equipment to keep me entertained. Then, at least when I went home alone I'd have fond memories of the evening.

By now, several of the other Dommes had walked back where the boys couldn't see us and wouldn't know who had claimed them. I tied a folded black bandana over the blond boy's eyes and clipped my leash to his collar.

"Thank you, Mistress," he whispered.

I had to take a deep breath and swallow hard to recover my equilibrium. I so missed hearing those words. *Enjoy the moment*, I told myself and patted him on the top of his head. His leash in one hand, I grabbed the duffle I keep my equipment in with the other. I led him to a table and guided him onto his back. With small, nylon pet collars and snap rings I fastened his wrists above his head and clipped them to two of the numerous eye bolts that protruded from the wooden edge of the padded table. I attached his ankles to the table so his knees faced the ceiling and his lovely, tight ass sat at the very edge, his big balls hanging down over his cheeks.

His bondage brought a smile to my lips -- boys look so lovely when they're helpless and vulnerable and this one was probably the prettiest toy available at the party. I made sure the blindfold didn't bind too tightly and grabbed a fistful of his silky hair. Bringing his ear up to my mouth, I asked: "What's your name, boy?"

"Eric, Mistress."

"What's your safeword?"

"Red will work fine, Mistress. Thank you."

I let his head drop back and ran my hand down his neck to his chest. The sparse, blond bristles of hair felt so different than Richard's dense, black fur. I missed having lots of chest hair to yank on, but relished the softer feel of skin against my palms.

The boy's splendid cock still stood erect, awaiting my attention. Although shorter than Richard's, it was significantly thicker. I drew one finger down the length and it twitched in response which made me smile again. I grabbed a bag of clothes pins and let them drop out onto Eric's stomach, knowing he would guess what I intended to do with them. One by one, I clipped them to his freshly shaved ball sack until all two dozen stuck out in every direction. Each clip brought a wince to the boy's face, and a "Thank you, Mistress" to his lips, but his cock remained upright. Richard, who had a very low pain tolerance, would have started screaming by now and wouldn't have stayed completely hard. This boy certainly seemed more fun to play with.

With another wicked grin, I ran my hand across the ends of the clothespins. His twisted grimace sent me looking in my bag for the metal "finger massagers" that I had purchased at a health food store. They look like springs soldered in a circle and I rolled one down the length of Eric's cock. He moaned. The thickness of his dick expanded the massagers much more than Richard's thin rod had. I imagined the metal pinched more. I placed a second massager around the shaft just under his cock head, watching to make sure it didn't constrict blood flow.

I had acquired my next implement from a kitchen outlet. After the dot-com bust a few years back, my employment situation suffered. Without much of a toy budget, I learned to find creative options in pet shops, hardware stores, and discount kitchen shops. When Richard left, he took most of the nicer toys he had bought me, so I was back to pervertibles. Designed for cutting pastry, the device I extracted from my bag has a metal wheel with a fluted edge. Not quite as painful as a Wartenberg wheel, but still quite effective, especially on a cock's sensitive skin. Licking my lips, I rolled it up and down the length of Eric's hard prick.

He moaned again and lifted his hips a little into my movement. I liked his reaction -- much more enjoyable than Richard's pleas for me to stop -- so I leaned over and kissed him. He responded hungrily, tasting my lips with his tongue. I had finally, after months of effort, taught Richard how to kiss sensuously. Despite being the same age, Eric didn't need any lessons.

When I got bored with the pastry wheel, I reached for a hair clip that had plastic nodules inside. I put that around Eric's cock between the massagers -- the teeth couldn't quite close -- engendering another moan. I leaned over, allowing my long hair to brush across Eric's chest so he would think I planned to kiss him again. This time I bit his nipple, hard. He squeaked. I bit the other one, pressing my teeth into his flesh until he yelped. I couldn't help chuckling -- pain tastes so good.

With one hand holding his cock up by the back of the clip, I flogged the exposed flesh with a small wire whisk, occasionally letting the metal strike his stomach or reaching over to hit his inner thighs. He wriggled his hips, but didn't make a sound. His skin reddened and my clit twitched.

I grabbed his hair again and whispered in his ear. "How're you doing, boy?"

"Fine, Mistress, thank you. You have unusual toys. I like them."

I laughed. Richard said my laugh had a wicked resonance that would shame Dorothy's nemesis. I watched Eric shiver at the sound, although I couldn't tell if fear or delight caused his reaction. I leaned over and pressed my teeth into the head of his cock until he screamed.

By now, I had pussy juice dripping down my thighs and I desperately needed some relief. I checked Eric's tag, then fumbled in my bag for a bottle of lube and my purple, vee-shaped, double-sided dildo. Pulling off my soaked thong, I slipped the egg-shaped knob of the shorter end inside my cunt, suppressing a gasp of delight. I slathered lube on the other, longer end that now protruded from my pubic hair. When I inserted gloved, lube-slick fingers inside the boy, he sucked in his breath and moaned. I panted with desire and need.

I slid the shaft into his sweet ass, the ribs at the base of the dildo where the two ends met rubbed against my clit, and I shuddered with orgasm. The boy sighed with obvious pleasure. Although he stole all the rest of my toys, Richard left my dildo behind. I assumed he did so because he hated taking it in the ass. I had derived some of my enjoyment from forcing him to accept something he disliked so much. But now I found myself relishing the big smile plastered across Eric's face. I slid in and out of him until I brought myself off again. I felt so good after that, I leaned over between his legs and planted a kiss on the top of his cock. It twitched and he moaned again. I had to wonder what it would feel like to sit on a rod that thick.

While I rested for a moment and enjoyed the aftershock spasms in my pussy, the surrounding activity penetrated my attention. Leather floggers whizzed through the air striking the skin of boys bound to crosses. A boy in a cage, with his ankles and legs trussed up behind his back, squealed as two women poked at him with bamboo canes. A woman in a black lace body stocking hit the bright red ass in front of her with a wooden paddle. Her boy, who was bent over one of the spanking benches, yelped and screeched.

Paula had bound her boy in the sling and penetrated him with a strapped-on dildo that made mine look minuscule. Barbara lay face down on a table with one boy massaging her back and another rubbing her feet. When she saw me looking her way, she winked at me. I couldn't see Angeline anywhere and guessed that she had taken her boy into one of the half dozen smaller, private rooms.

Steadying myself on my feet, I slid the dildo out of Eric's ass and my cunt, dropped it into a plastic bag, and trashed the gloves. Then, I lifted Eric's soft blond hair away from the sheen of perspiration on his face. "You still game, boy?" Richard would have begged me to stop twenty minutes ago and I wondered if Eric hadn't had anyone play with him in a long time. Shame if a boy this pretty couldn't find an owner. But maybe he was just a pain slut, not interested in submitting beyond the bedroom or the party.

"Perhaps Mistress would care to try some of the other activities listed on my tag?" His voice had a tight edge to it and I admired him for not safe-wording me. I kissed him again, this time thrusting my tongue deep into his mouth and letting it dance with his.

When I removed the hair clip, he whimpered. Each clothespin came off with a sob and my pussy got wetter. I rolled the finger massagers off his cock, slowly to maximize the pain, and he groaned.

"Thank you, Mistress," he whispered. I stroked the soft, now-naked flesh. "You have lovely fingers."

I wrapped those "lovely fingers" around his shaft and squeezed until he groaned again. Then I ran a hand across his muscular chest. *I wish I could take this one home*, I thought to myself. Maybe, like Richard, he appreciated an older Mistress.

After gathering up my toys, I unclipped the collars around his wrists and ankles from the eyebolts on the table, and watched amused as the boy struggled, while still blindfolded, to clean off the padding with a wipe I had found in a canister on one of the tables set around the room. Then, I led him by the leash over to an empty spanking bench. *No reason not to enjoy playing with this toy as long as I can.*

Eric kneeled on the bench and bent his chest over the padded top. I clipped his arms to eyebolts near the base and he let his head hang down, ready to take whatever I chose to inflict on him. I caressed his fine, tight ass with my hand, reveling in the firmness. Alternating between a leather belt Richard had left behind and a wooden spoon, I walloped Eric's backside until it had a nice, red glow and the ache in my pussy had become unbearable. I unclipped the boy's wrists, stuffed everything in my duffle, and led him by the leash over to one of the sofas along the far wall. Paula sat at one end, her boy kneeling in front of her, kissing her feet and sucking on her toes. She gave me an intoxicated smile. I settled on the other end and pulled on the leash until my boy lowered himself to his knees. I grabbed his hair to tilt his head back and kissed him.

I wanted to push his face between my legs, but he hadn't put oral worship on his tag so I pulled the bandana blindfold off his face and leaned back. The boy gave me a long, lingering glance, taking in tits pushed up and waist pinched small by the corset. Although he didn't raise his eyes to my face, I could see him checking out my pale skin and green eyes through his long blond lashes.

To my surprise, a smile brightened his face and he leaned over to kiss my hand. "If I may say so, Mistress is quite beautiful. I hope she isn't done playing with me, yet."

"Hardly," I laughed, giddy at the thought that this beautiful boy found me attractive. I looped one leg around the back of his neck and urged him forward, hoping the missing activity was just an oversight. He didn't require more prompting than that, lifting my skirt and kissing his way up the inside of my thigh. I settled back into the cushions while he licked the juices off my pubic hair and then worked his tongue inside my slit. A moan escaped me when he slid it across my clit and it didn't take long for him to bring me off.

That didn't slow him down. "Mistress tastes so very good." He lapped up the extra juices and sucked and licked until I came again and again. I had to give the boy credit for perceptiveness. He quickly figured out what I liked best and the orgasms became more and more intense until I had to take a break.

I pulled his hair, dragging his head out from under my skirt and bringing him up on the sofa next to me. Kissing him, I tasted myself on his full lips. I stroked his silky hair with one hand, slid my other down his back, and allowed him to slip his arms around my waist. It felt so good to have a boy in my arms again, even if only for the evening. That, combined with the glow from countless orgasms, made me wish the boy were available..

Releasing his lips, I guided his head onto my shoulder. We sat there for a long bit, while I played with his hair and ran my hand along his back. But, instead of asking directly about his ownership status, I put the ball in his court. "Tell me about yourself, boy."

"Not much to tell, really." He shifted his head so his lips touched my neck and his hot breath tickled my skin. "I'm a computer programmer. I own a small house on the northeast side and I'm building a dungeon in the basement. I've had four or five years' lifestyle experience. What else would Mistress like to know?"

May as well go for broke. "Do you have an owner? Are you looking for one?"

"I regret to say I've never found a woman I wanted to belong to who thought me worthy of her collar. I would very much like to." He reached out with his tongue and, without moving his head, licked the length of my neck. That and his words sent a shiver down my spine. "May I ask if Mistress is in the market for a pet?"

I managed to suppress a gasp and respond with more

calmness than I felt. "As a matter of fact, I am." I ran my fingers through his hair. "But, I need more than just a play toy."

"I'm very obedient, Ma'am. I've had training as both a houseboy and a sex toy." He slipped out of my arms, onto his knees, and lay his head on my thigh. "I earn a nice living, I've tried to create a home that a woman would enjoy living in, and I make a very presentable escort in vanilla circumstances. I don't smoke or do drugs, and I only drink alcohol in moderation."

I patted the top of his head, trying to maintain my composure. "You certainly seem to have all the qualities I would want in a pet. Of course, a long-term relationship requires compatibility and chemistry as well."

"If Mistress will permit me to say so," he pushed my skirt back far enough to kiss the inside of my knees, "at least on my part, the chemistry is quite strong. I hope, since Mistress chose this boy to play with, she finds his appearance acceptable."

I laughed. I couldn't believe this boy would consider giving himself to me after one encounter, but I had never met a boy I wanted to own so much. "More than acceptable." I grabbed his hair, pulled his head back, and kissed him. "You're downright adorable."

When I released him, he said, "Thank you, Mistress. May I ask, have you ever owned a slave?"

I bit my lip to keep back the tears and waited until I could speak without my voice shaking. "I collared a boy a year and a half ago. He left me four months back. Like so many, he claimed to want complete control, but then tried to top from the bottom and complained about my restrictions."

"Mistress, I can assure you that should you ever find me worthy of your collar, I would never presume to question your authority or give you anything less than my total devotion. But, the truth is it's just as difficult to find a woman willing to take complete control of a man. I don't want to be someone's partner, I want to be her slave."

I closed my eyes and wondered if I could ever put my collar around another boy's neck. Richard's desertion had devastated me. Still, I knew I didn't want to live alone. And this boy seemed to have everything I could possibly want: he learned fast, seemed to understand the owner/slave dynamic, had a nice build, tolerated lots of pain, and knew what to do with his tongue. But what did he see in me?

I heard a door open across the room and saw Angeline step out leading a boy on a leash, following her on all fours. She had a glazed look in her eyes. I stood up and tugged on my own leash. The boy grabbed my duffle and I took him into the small room furnished only with a bed that had eye hooks along the top and bottom rails. Whatever came of this night, I wanted to enjoy everything this boy had to offer.

I locked the door and waited while Eric put clean sheets on the bed from the stack on the wooden shelf above the headboard. When he turned around to face me, I pushed on his chest until he sat down. Throwing one leg over his, I straddled his thighs and pulled him against my breast. I ran my fingers through his hair, kissed him then guided his mouth down my neck to my tits. He covered them in kisses, licking and caressing them with his lips. I could have purred. Richard was a leg and foot man and had to be reminded to give my jugs the attention they craved. When Eric finally lifted one tit reverently from my corset so he could wrap his lips around my nipple, I almost came from the delicious sensation it sent to my clit.

When I couldn't bear the tension any longer, I shoved him back on the bed and guided him into a position where I could clip his wrists to the top rail. At that point, I didn't have the patience to worry about securing his ankles. I crawled up over his shoulders and sat on his face, dripping my juices all over him. With his tongue flicking everywhere I wanted it, I came three times before I eased myself down over his chest and stuffed his cock up inside me.

Damn, he feels good there. I discovered thick had definite advantages over long. I rode Eric for nearly twenty minutes, until I could see a drop of blood where he bit into his lip. "You may come now, boy."

His blue eyes twinkled with relief and excitement. "Thank you so much, Mistress." Didn't take the boy more than three strokes to finish off with a grunt and I wondered how long he could have held out. Richard would have begged for permission long before now.

When Eric stopped spurting, I unclipped his wrists and rolled over on my back next to him. "Clean up your mess, boy."

"Yes, Mistress; thank you Mistress." He crawled toward the foot of the bed and lapped and sucked all his jism from my bush and my cunt, bringing me off another couple of times in the process.

I grabbed his hair and pulled him up so he could lay with his head on my shoulder. I stroked the skin of his muscular arms and back while I floated in post-orgasmic euphoria. For the first time, I rejoiced in Richard's departure. Barbara was right, that fool didn't deserve me. "Well, boy, if your house-keeping skills prove as good as your abilities as a sex toy, I might just have to collar you."

"Oh, Mistress, thank you. Nothing would make me happier than to be owned by such a beautiful and Dominant woman. I just know you could truly take complete owner-ship of me." He lifted his head enough to kiss the shoulder that had cradled it. I grabbed his hair and pulled his lips to mine.

Acknowledgements

This book would not have reached your hands without the help of many dear friends and colleagues. I thank my readers and supporters, especially Cindy, my proofreader, editor, and best friend. Thanks also to all those who have served me, well and ill, over the years. I have learned something from each one of you and I hope that you find what you seek.

Other fiction

by I.G. Frederick includes:

Complicated Couplings

Four sexy stories about tangled twosomes

"If You Love Someone" — *Tara leaves her husband to move in with Nathan, but he abandons her after a few months. When he returns, begging her to take him back, life and love look very different.*

"Commiserate" — *The same man dumped them both. When they commiserate, they discover more in common than an ex-boyfriend.*

"Passion's Price" — *Richard steals Gina's heart from three thousand miles away. But, when he moves across the country, her intensity and passion for life drive him away.*

"Lunchtime Lover" — *Both married, they started their affair with the promise never to fall in love. Then Lisa's divorce becomes final.*

www.eroticawriter.net/ComplicatedCouplings.html

Cougar Conquests

Beautiful older women on the prowl and the sweet young cubs captured by their allure

"Benjamin" — A chance meeting at a munch in a tiny town leads Benjamin to an opportunity for training. But, Lady Gina tries to end the relationship rather than emotionally torture herself.

"Festival of Eros" — The handsome young man followed her around all evening, behaving like the perfect submissive ... until she learned his identity.

"Paddles" — A biker bar with no bikers? The decor, name, and patrons of a bar in a small Eastern Oregon town puzzle William who just stopped in for a beer. Then the owner introduces him to the secrets of this very special tavern.

"Starting Over" - When her pet walked out on her, she stayed away from parties because it hurt to watch other women playing with their toys. But, a friend coerces her into attending a unique event.

"The Cougar and the College Boys" — Alone in the woods, hours from Portland, Tess discovers four college friends staying in a nearby cabin. The boys invite her to share their campfire, their dinner, and ...

www.eroticawriter.net/CougarConquests.html

Dommemoir

WARNING:
This book changes women's attitudes about relationship dynamics, forever.

In Geneviéve's journey of discovery she dabbles in the BDSM lifestyle which forces her to recognize and acknowledge her true nature. Her memoir, woven together with that of a male slave, draws the reader into an intense odyssey of sexual expression triumphing over sexual repression while delivering fascinating insight about a different kind of love.

"The aptly titled Dommemoir *delivers on so many levels... It quickly sucks you in and envelopes you in the bondage of its spell...* Dommemoir *is a character study that breathes complex and compelling life into its hero, the devastating Lady Geneviéve and the fortunate submissives who worship at her feet... placing you in the delicious bondage of its dark and compelling landscape..."*

Larry Brooks, USA Today bestselling author of Darkness Bound **and** Bait and Switch

www.eroticawriter.net/Dommemoir.html

Eleanor & Mick

A journey of sexual exploration and insight

In five sizzling hot stories, Eleanor seeks refuge in a small town on the Oregon Coast and befriends her younger neighbor. He captures first her heart and then her submission, taking her on a journey of sexual exploration and insight.

"Salt for His Wounds" — When Eleanor's ex-husband shows up begging for a second chance, she asks her young, gorgeous next door neighbor for a favor and Mick takes advantage of the opportunity.

"The Mercantile" — Eleanor attributes Mick's detachment to the difference in their ages, but Mick confesses a need for kink. Afraid of losing him, Eleanor reluctantly consents to bondage and pain.

"The Things We Do for Love" — When her gorgeous girlfriend visits Eleanor on the coast, Mick's obvious attraction troubles her. But, Liz only has eyes for Eleanor.

"Paid in Full" — Mick's army buddy finds Eleanor hot and makes a deal with Mick. But, if Mick really loved Eleanor would he let another man have sex with her?

"Renovations" — After Mick spends a month renovating their garage, Eleanor discovers he built in a few surprises.

www.eroticawriter.net/EleanorMick.html

Family Dynamics

Six sultry stories exploring sexuality in Dominant/submissive liaisons

"'Aunt' Grace" — Jen needed a place to stay in Portland and turned to her father's stepsister. But, she found so much more than she ever dreamed possible with her "Aunt" Grace. Second Place, NLA:I John Preston Short Story Award.

"Leather Family" — Kyle needs his own boy. Jacques would do almost anything to find a place in a Leather Family. But, Kyle serves a female Master.

"Searching"— Two dominants love each other, but need someone who submits to them both. Just how far will young Jeremy go to serve the lovely Lady Theresa?

"Taking Control" — To free the woman she loves from a horrid sadist's perverted games, Melanie must set aside her own aversion to men.

"Family Ties" — When her slave's ex faces eviction, Katherine offers refuge. But can Naomi pay the price?

"Said the Unicorn" — Tessa dedicates herself to her Master's service, so his determination to add another woman to their family devastates her.

www.eroticawriter.net/FamilyDynamics.html

Fork In The Road

Changing people's lives, and relationships
in three pairs of sexy stories

"*Said the Unicorn*" — *Tessa dedicates herself to her Master's service, so his determination to add another woman to their family devastates her.*

"*Proposals*" — *The evening appears perfectly arranged for him to pop the question. But, Christopher's proposition takes Geraldine on an unanticipated sexual adventure.*

"*Winners & Losers*" — *When he finally walks away from the blackjack table, Jeffrey finds someone worth gambling on.*

www.eroticawriter.net/ForkinRoad.html

Ladies in Love

Six sizzling stories of Lesbian Lust

"*Empty Seat*" — *Laura offers Alex a nightcap as thanks for help with a presentation to a prospective client. But they never order drinks.*

"*'Aunt' Grace*" — *Jen needed a place to stay in Portland and turned to her father's stepsister. But, she* found so much more than she ever dreamed possible with her "Aunt" Grace. Second Place, National Leather Association: International John Preston Short Story Award.

"Spa Date" — Dismayed that she introduced Sam to the woman who betrayed her, Julie tries to fix her up again.

"Taking Control" — To free the woman she loves from a horrid sadist's perverted games, Melanie must set aside her own aversion to men.

"Dental School" — How can Cindy flirt with the beautiful blonde dental instructor while her mother propositions the student examining her teeth on Cindy's behalf?

"Commiserate" — The same man dumped them both. When they commiserate, they discover more in common than an ex-boyfriend.

www.eroticawriter.net/LadiesinLove.html

Lessons Learned
Sometimes you need more than love

Four sizzling hot FemDom love stories about women who come to terms with their dominant sides and discover that makes them more attractive to the men they love.

"Tea Party" — What if the first time your best friend drags you to a FemDom "Tea Party" you see your former boyfriend serving canapes naked?

"Blind Date" — How do you respond when you find your ex-husband hanging out at the restaurant where you planned to meet your "Blind Date"?

"To Serve" — If you love a vanilla woman and you only want "To Serve," how do you introduce her to the lifestyle without scaring her away?

"Change in View" — What if a "Change in View" alters the attitude of the man you mentored so he could find his perfect Mistress?

www.eroticawriter.net/LessonsLearned.html

Love Hurts
but in a good way

five steamy stories about the dark side of love

"B&D Trainee" — Online, Xavier promised to make his B&D fantasies come true. But, had he jumped in over his head?

"Knife Play" — Seeking a knife he saw online, Jack inadvertently found himself in a room full of pain and bondage contraptions. He almost turned around and

left, but a beautiful woman taught him a different way to appreciate blades.

"Pussy Whipped" — Eric knew nothing about BDSM, but purchased a ticket to a fundraiser to help out his friends. When Miranda asks him to "play," he discovers exactly what those four letters mean.

"The Auction" — He attended the auction with only one goal — to acquire a very special whip. But an offer to try it out proved irresistible and he discovered sometimes events, and women, can exceed one's expectations.

"FemDom Fairy Tale" — A FemDom's offhand remark about a photograph at an erotic art show draws a handsome man's attention. But, when two dominants find each other attractive, which one chooses to kneel?

www.eroticawriter.net/LoveHurts.html

When Two's Not Enough

Seven sexy ménage stories

"Tribal Fusion" — Whenever and wherever he dances, Dominic collects propositions, but the Lady Lenore's proposal takes him by surprise.

"Two Brothers" — A divorcée in a flashy sports car attracts the attention of two young virgin brothers visiting the "big" city of Boise.

"Honeymoon" — Although she expected to honeymoon aboard a cruise ship, Allison finds herself sailing on a private yacht staffed by an incredibly beautiful couple. Believing her new husband wants to hide his older, less attractive wife, makes it difficult to enjoy the hedonistic delights offered in paradise.

"Jail Bait" — Serena wants Joshua to pop her cherry, but he won't touch her because of her age. When her birthday finally makes it legal, he arranges for a very special celebration.

"Nikki's Birthday" — Even someone happy in a monogamous relationship might find the gift of a hot, new toy for an evening of decadence incredibly exciting. (Inspired by a real birthday present given to a lovely little bi-sexual, genderqueer slave.)

"Market Boy" — When a beautiful Domme offers Jack the opportunity to serve at a party for her friends, he responds too quickly and too eagerly, getting more than he bargained for.

"The Cougar and the College Boys" — Alone in the woods, hours from Portland, Tess discovers four college friends staying in a nearby cabin. The boys invite her to share their campfire, their dinner, and ...

www.eroticawriter.net/TwoNotEnough.html

Young & Eager

Barely legal but hardly innocent

"Two Brothers" — *A divorcée in a flashy sports car attracts the attention of two young virgin brothers visiting the "big" city of Boise.*

"Teachers Pet" — *Trapped at an all-girls' school in the middle of nowhere, Sabrina tries to get her hunky teacher to bust her cherry.*

"Arresting Development" — *Bethany went out with Officer Rick to avoid a speeding ticket, but discovered she enjoyed getting "arrested."*

"Jail Bait" — *Serena wants Joshua to pop her cherry, but he won't touch her because of her age. When her birthday finally makes it legal, he arranges for a very special celebration.*

www.eroticawriter.net/YoungEager.html

Or visit
http://eroticawriter.net/
to find links to individual stories
and additional collections
and